SATAN'S SHORTS

HEIDE GOODY

IAIN GRANT

IF YOU'VE NOT READ CLOVENHOOF BEFORE…

The one-handed man writhed in the chunky armchair as he struggled to find the words to express himself. Waiting patiently for him to find those words, Denise silently chided herself for regarding him once again as 'the one-handed man'. Mr Dewsbury was much more than his outer appearance. Her role as a person-centred therapist – as Sutton Coldfield's eminent person-centred therapist - was to see the bigger picture, see the whole person.

Well, not the whole person in Mr Dewsbury's case. What was he? Ninety-five percent whole? Ninety-seven? How much was a hand, percentage-wise?

"The devil is living in my flat," said Mr Dewsbury.

Five percent? Three? A hand might be important but it's not that big.

Mr Dewsbury coughed loudly.

"Did you hear what I said?"

Denise blinked and then smiled.

"Sorry, I was thinking about what you said before."

Mr Dewsbury frowned.

"I didn't say anything before."

"No. But what did you say just then?"

"The devil is living in *my* flat."

"There's a devil in your flat."

"Not *a* devil. *The* devil. Satan. Beelzebub. Lucifer."

"Oh, and do you see him in your flat?"

"No. I don't see him there."

"He's just a presence, is he? A feeling?"

"No, I don't see him because I don't live there anymore."

"Why not?"

"Because *he* does. He moved in last year. There's only one bedroom. We're not... you know. We don't... cohabit."

"And this is the devil, is it?" she asked.

Mr Dewsbury nodded vigorously.

"Satan," he said.

"Beelzebub."

"Lucifer."

She nodded in a reassuring manner she had practised in front of the mirror.

"Do tell me, Mr Dewsbury, why is Satan living in Birmingham? I mean it's a lovely place but..."

"He lost his job."

"As the devil?"

"As ruler of Hell. And then he was evicted."

"Right. And so he chose to relocate to the West Midlands."

"No," scowled Mr Dewsbury. "He was sent here."

"Why here?"

Mr Dewsbury sighed and jiggled his head.

"I may have suggested it to the archangels."

"Oh, so you see angels too?"

"Not anymore," he said. "You see, I used to be dead."

"But you're not now, are you?"

"No, I'm not," he said grumpily. "I was happy in heaven."

"I hear it's nice."

"Are you mocking me?"

Denise shook her head gently.

"I do not mock my clients, Mr Dewsbury. I'm here to support you through this situation."

"Okay," he said, mildly mollified. "I was dead. I wasn't using my flat at the time. I thought it ideal. And, besides, Satan and my old neighbours..."

"What is it, Mr Dewsbury?"

"Well, frankly, they deserve each other. The man across the hall, Ben Kitchen, is a weirdo."

"Weirdo?"

"A grown man, spending all his time cooped up with his computers and his little toy soldiers when he's not slobbing about that so-called bookshop of his. Not married, you know. I'd assume he was a poofter but at least the gays have the decency to iron their shirts and run a hoover round the place every now and then. And the woman upstairs..."

"You don't get on with one another?"

"Nerys Thomas has so many men coming in and out of her flat that she ought to install a turnstile. No sense of decency or shame that woman."

Denise, who had her own views of homosexuality,

decency and a woman's right to live how she damn well pleased, kept her thoughts and emotions hidden.

"And these two people have Satan for a neighbour."

"Yes. Well, he goes by the name of Jeremy Clovenhoof these days. His secret identity."

"So, he's just an ordinary man to look at, is he?"

"No!" said Mr Dewsbury with fresh venom. "He's got the horns, the hooves, the red skin, the lot."

"Really?"

"Really."

"Don't people notice this? Aren't they surprised?"

"They don't notice!" squeaked Mr Dewsbury, a frantic edge entering his voice and his eyes. "They can't see it!"

"So everyone else thinks he's just a man."

"Everyone except the barman at the Boldmere Oak."

"What?" said Denise.

"Lennox the barman. He knows."

"How come he can tell that Jeremy Clovenhoof is Satan when no one else can?"

"I don't know!" squealed Mr Dewsbury. "I'm not making this up!"

"Of course not," said Denise in soothing tones.

Mr Dewsbury buried his head into his one hand and sobbed softly.

"What am I to do?"

Denise picked up her personal planner from the coffee table.

"I think we need to book another session," she said.

Mr Dewsbury looked at her from between his fingers.

"Probably quite a few," she said, giving him a little smile.

1

———————

CLOVENHOOF GOES TO NIGHT SCHOOL

Ben, Nerys and Clovenhoof met on the steps of the Paradise Adult Education Centre, their breath misting in the chill night air.

Clovenhoof gazed at the orange sodium glare of the street lights on Paradise Street and tried to pretend, unsuccessfully, that he was gazing at the cleansing fires of the Old Place.

"Well, that was a load of bollocks," he said with quiet sincerity.

"What are you talking about?" said Nerys, opening her handbag to look for her car keys. "I thought there was a lot on offer there. Art, languages, computing. Although I'll tell you what, that woman should *not* be allowed to teach yoga."

"I enjoyed the yoga," said Clovenhoof. "Very relaxing."

"Yeah, a bit too relaxed, Jeremy. Certain muscles should always remain clenched."

"Better out than in," said Clovenhoof and cracked his knuckles.

"What was wrong with the yoga instructor?" asked Ben.

"Cellulite," said Nerys. "More orange peel than the fake fruit that Jeremy tried to eat."

"And why," said Ben, turning to Clovenhoof, "was this evening a load of... rubbish?"

"I was mis-sold, time and again." He counted his grievances off on his fingers. "First of all, it was supposed to be a night-school taster session. I didn't get to eat anything. That wax fruit! What the hell is that about? And the art dude had the nerve to be upset with *me*. Secondly, the pottery woman tells us we're going to throw pots and gets all shirty when I do. And book-keeping!"

"I might sign up for the book-keeping," said Ben. "A bit of a refresher, like."

"Where were the books?" said Clovenhoof. "Not much of a book-keeper if he hasn't got any books left."

"Now, you know it doesn't mean-"

"It's almost as bad as that bookmaker's on the high street. They don't make any! I used to pop in every day just to see if I could catch them at it. Not that I'm allowed in there anymore."

"Why not?"

"The 3:15 at Market Rasen last month. A horse called My Face. I got over-excited. I don't want to talk about it."

"You're too wound up. That's your problem," said Nerys still ferreting around for her keys.

"I signed up for the meditation course," Clovenhoof agreed.

"You?" said Ben. "Meditation?"

"You don't think I can handle a meditation course?"

"I don't think meditation can handle you, my friend."

"I thought you were going to go for something more... academic," said Nerys. "Isn't that why we came here? All those educational supplies you came home with the other day. We talked. Remember?"

Clovenhoof made a noise in his throat. Yes, he had returned to the flat with reams of notepaper, three folders, an academic diary and a Hello Kitty stationery kit. Yes, Nerys had seen them and then *she* had talked. And talked. And produced an Adult Education prospectus from somewhere. Clovenhoof didn't get a word in edgeways at any point, and did not have time to regale her with the tale of his trip to the stationers which featured a long queue, boredom, an electric pencil sharpener that gave the patently false impression of being custom-made for sharpening dull horns, an unexpected electrical fault, a broken till, some shouting and Clovenhoof running out with anything he could lay his hands on, leaving the stationer with as much money as he felt he owed her (seventy-three pence and an old betting slip).

"I think I'm a bit beyond the need for schooling," said Clovenhoof witheringly.

"Oh, we can all do with a little self-improvement," said Ben.

"Not me." Clovenhoof puffed out his chest and tucked his thumbs into his waistcoat pockets. "When He made me, He broke the mould. One of a kind."

"Got them!" declared Nerys, victoriously holding the car keys aloft.

"Oh! And another thing!" said Clovenhoof, returning to

an earlier theme as they walked towards the car. "Knight school? I didn't see a sword or scrap of plate armour anywhere."

"Now you're being silly," said Ben. "Although, thinking about it, I'd sign up for a class like that."

He drew an imaginary sword from an equally imaginary scabbard with a metallic "Shing!"

"You'd be gutted in an instant," said Clovenhoof, drawing his own pretend blade.

"Really, boys?" said Nerys. "Here? In public?"

"Fear not, fair maiden," declared Clovenhoof. "It will be over in but a mo-"

Clovenhoof, drawing his arm back to deliver a skull-cleaving blow, punched a passerby cleanly in the jaw. The bearded fellow went down hard on the tarmac.

"See, that's what happens when you behave like idiots," said Nerys.

Clovenhoof looked down at the felled man. Ben offered the man a hand.

"You all right, sir?"

Clutching his jaw, the man furiously waved the hand away and, through his pain, growled, "*Pedicabo ego vos et irrumabo!*"

"What did he say?" asked Ben.

"He... politely declines your offer of assistance," said Clovenhoof.

"He looks like he might need first aid," said Nerys hopefully.

The man got to his feet and staggered away, moaning and swearing under his breath.

"Home then," said Nerys, mildly disappointed that she didn't get a chance to showcase her first aid skills.

"Do I have to sit in the back again?" said Ben.

"I did call shotgun," said Clovenhoof.

"When?"

"Then."

"Well, can we at least take the child lock off the back door?"

AT NIGHT SCHOOL the following week, Nerys found herself regretting signing up for the 'painting from life' class.

The art teacher, Patty, a large woman who at least had the decency to hide her calorific sins beneath a paint-spattered artist's smock, had set the dozen-or-so students the uninspiring task of sketching plants and fruit. Nerys had been given a square of cardboard, a selection of pencils and a tiny cactus.

She stared at it for a long time.

"Thinking of how to approach it?" said Patty.

"It's a bloody cactus. I'm not sure *why* I'd want to draw it."

"It's a challenge, isn't it?" said Patty. "Very difficult to convey."

Ben, who had signed up for the same class, seemed unaccountably content with drawing an apple. He bent over his work, pencil moving intermittently yet confidently across the card. There was a look of passionate concentration on his face that Nerys felt a mere apple did not deserve.

She stared at her cactus again. Fine, she thought.

She sketched the pot first, oval upon oval, joined by

vertical lines. It was a bit wobbly but would suffice. She drew the outline of the cactus and then stopped to appraise what she had committed to paper. It looked less like a cactus than a cucumber or an inexplicably potted sausage. In an attempt to make good this disturbing image, she quickly pencilled in the cactus's spines. It was not an improvement. It looked like a hairy cucumber now.

"Cocks!" she said under her breath and turned her cardboard over.

Through two sets of windows, Nerys could see into an empty classroom across the corridor where a tall houseplant with dark waxy leaves stood.

"Now, *that's* a proper plant," she said.

"Hmm?" said Ben not looking up.

She looked at his drawing. With light shading and a bit a thumb-smudging, he'd somehow managed to convey the roundness of the fruit, its sheen and luscious swell.

"Nothing, apple-boy," she said, hopping off her stool and out of the door.

The other classroom door was unlocked and she slipped inside. It was a science classroom with rows of high benches studded with gas taps. In one corner, a range of plants and glass tanks clustered beneath a mural of a rainforest. The plant she had spotted from afar was a good two feet tall, its leaves fat and firm.

Smiling at her own good taste, Nerys gripped the plant pot and slid it off the work surface. It was heavy and she grunted as she took its weight in her hands.

From the biggest tank a large snake with mottled brown scales watched her.

"I'm only borrowing it," she told the snake.

The snake's tongue flicked out for an instant but it passed no further comment.

With leaves in her eyes and the awkward weight of the plant straining her fingertips, Nerys backed out into the classroom, across the corridor and pushed the next door open with her back. She turned and, through the foliage, saw that she had wandered into the wrong classroom.

"Oh," she said and put the houseplant down on the edge of a desk.

Eight pairs of eyes were on her, middle-aged men and women sat expectantly at the rows of the desks set before the whiteboard. There was no lecturer at the front of the room.

"Teacher not here?" she said as she tried to blow some life back into her fingertips.

A thickset man at the back made a displeased noise and another said, "I heard Dr Wiles was attacked in the car park last week."

"Someone dislocated his jaw, I heard," piped up a woman in an unflattering cardigan.

Nerys frowned.

"Bald bloke? Scruffy beard? Swears in Latin?"

"That's him," said cardigan woman.

"I think I've met him," said Nerys.

"So are you our replacement for the evening?" said a man.

"We've been waiting for half an hour," said cardigan woman.

The thickset man made another noise of displeasure.

A bespectacled man at the front laughed lightly.

"I don't think this young woman knows much about classical languages," he said. "No offence meant, child."

"Child?" Nerys cleared her throat. "And what's your name?"

"Adrian," he said blithely.

"Well, Adrian..."

Nerys looked at the assembled students, eight adults with attentive eyes only for her. She looked at the pile of text books on the edge of the teacher's desk. A little voice in her head screamed, "Don't do it, Nerys. Just kick him in the babymaker, treat the ageist chauvinist to the scolding of his life and leave" but it was only a little voice.

"Nil desperandum, class. Your teacher is here at last," she said and began to dish out the text books.

In a corridor in another part of the Paradise Adult Education Centre, Clovenhoof was not taking rejection well.

"But I was really enjoying it," he said.

The meditation instructor pulled the classroom door closed behind her and stepped into the corridor.

"You're distracting the other students, Mr Clovenhoof. The guided meditation -"

"Was great. I really felt like I was floating, high above the clouds."

"Is that why you were making aeroplane noises?"

He winced.

"Just got a bit carried away."

"I'm sorry. I don't think it's going to work out."

"But I'm *this* close to enlightenment. I can feel it."

"I'll speak to the office staff about refunding your registration fee. I'm sorry," she said and retreated inside the classroom once more, closing the door firmly behind her.

"I bet the Buddha didn't have to put up with this," he said loudly and stomped down the corridor, deliberately scuffing his hooves on the parquet flooring.

"Of course, he didn't need a bloody meditation class," he muttered to himself. "Just found himself a tree to sit under and waited for enlightenment to hit him on the head like an apple." He paused. "Or was that Isaac Newton?"

Through the open door of an empty classroom, he espied a mural of thrusting tropical trees and with treeish thoughts in his head, went inside.

"I don't need their stinking classes," he said. "I could just sit here and wait for universal wisdom to descend on me."

He looked at the fat brown reticulated python in the glass tank beneath the mural.

"How's the wisdom business, o subtlest and craftiest of beasts?"

The serpent was silent.

"Wisest thing I've heard all day," said Clovenhoof.

Without a moment's hesitation, he removed the tank lid and lifted the snake out. He rested its fat, smooth coils across his shoulders. The python languidly tightened its grip around his arms. He smiled at the comforting weight and pressure.

"You know, I spent some time as a serpent," said Clovenhoof. "Long time ago now. I was happy then. For a while."

He absent-mindedly caressed the snake's skin.

"Not a big fan of crawling on your belly in the dust, mind. Legs are good things. I'd recommend legs."

He paused. There seemed to be some raised voices coming from a classroom across the way and, unless he was mistaken, he recognised one of them.

"Excuse me," he said, quickly but carefully returning the snake to its tank, and crossed the corridor to the noisy classroom.

Nerys, who, for some reason that would no doubt become clear, stood in front of a class of balding and sagging pupils, one of whom seemed terribly upset with her board work. On the board were the words, *cogito ergo sum*.

"I just want to know how to conjugate the verb to be?" said the annoyed little man.

"Why would you want to conjugate it?" said Nerys.

"Is it an irregular verb?"

Nerys looked at the board.

"Does it look irregular to you?"

"I don't know," said the man, his spectacles vibrating with irritation. "You tell me."

"Can we perhaps tell by context?"

"No, Professor Thomas, we can't."

"*Professor* Thomas?" said Clovenhoof.

Nerys saw him for the first time and an expression of panic mixed with embarrassment flooded her face.

"Oh, hi. Do you know any Latin, by any chance?"

"I dabble," said Clovenhoof. "Una lingua numquam satis est."

"Indeed," said Nerys. "*Doctor* Clovenhoof, I was just explaining to Adrian here that we don't need to get too hung up on the technical details. We must walk before we can run. QED. *That's* Latin, that is."

"I just wanted to know the conjugation of the verb," said Adrian in a petulant staccato.

Clovenhoof cleared his throat.

"Sum, I am. Es, you are, singular. Est, he or she is. Sumus, we are. Estis, you are, plural. Sunt, they are."

"Ah-hah. See, Adrian?" said Nerys. "Easy. Surprised you didn't know that. As they say in Rome... er... dôs adra i farw i'r gath gael bwyd."

"That sounded Welsh to me," said a woman at the back.

"Ha ha!" laughed Nerys. "As if. Perhaps you'd like to take over from here, Dr Clovenhoof."

Clovenhoof gave her a broad grin.

"Recedite, plebes," he said, taking centre stage. "Let the education begin."

BEN STOOD IN THE REFECTORY, sipping an uninspiring cup of vending machine coffee and reading health and safety notices on the wall as he waited for Nerys and Clovenhoof to appear. Nerys had failed to return to the art room after going off in a huff and there was no sign of Clovenhoof in the meditation class. The instructor had given Ben a filthy look when he mentioned Clovenhoof's name and he beat a swift retreat. Now, with all the classes over and the caretakers locking doors and turning off the lights, Ben was left alone with his coffee sludge, information on how best to tackle asbestos in the workplace and the unshakeable child-like fear that he had somehow been abandoned.

"Excuse me," said a voice behind him, "do you know w-"

Ben turned and all but impaled himself on the young woman's umbrella. His hand went instinctively to his speared ribs, flung coffee all down his front and then, in the ensuing sweary chaos, dropped his art folder and almost head-butted the health and safety notice board.

"Oh, God. I'm sorry," said the woman, casting her umbrella aside and crouching to pick up Ben's scattered artwork. The woman's long multi-coloured scarf – which either indicated an aren't-I-kooky-and-bohemian personality or an unhealthy obsession with Tom Baker's Doctor Who – pooled on the floor at her feet.

Ben opened his mouth to speak, coughed at the pain in his side and waved his hand to generally indicate his thanks and that she should continue picking up papers.

"These are good," she said, standing up.

"No," said Ben, who was horrified that someone should be looking at his artwork, particularly the enthusiastic little sketches he had done between signing up for the art course and this first lesson.

"They are," she said, smiling as she put the papers back in the art folder. Her smile was wide, unreserved and entirely natural. Ben didn't get treated to many smiles like that.

"I particularly like this one," she said and tapped her finger on the topmost paper, a pencil sketch Ben had made of one of his wargaming miniatures.

"Really?" he said.

"Alexandrine isn't it?"

"Close," said Ben, impressed. "Seleucid actually. A chalkaspides."

"Oh, I don't know so much about them. Early Hellenic history is really my thing. But I love that kind of historical setting. There's something honest about it, not simple but somehow...real. Back in the days when men were real men and bestrode the world like colossi."

Her fingers touched the Seleucidian warrior's muscles, the honed body that Ben himself had meticulously drawn. He found himself viewing the picture anew and felt a bizarre and almost uncontrollable desire to shout, "I'm not gay!"

Instead he thrust his hand out at her.

"I'm Ben," he said.

"Felicity," she replied, shaking his hand and treating him to another beautiful smile. Ben thought he could get used to a smile like that.

"So you're a bit of an ancient history buff?" he said.

"Ancient history *student*," said Felicity. "Doing my masters in Birmingham. I also work part time at the museum and art gallery."

"That sounds like a dream job to me."

"Ah, it doesn't pay much. I have to find extra ways to make ends meet. Speaking of which... I was going to ask you if you knew where the art rooms were. I'm looking for a teacher called Patty."

"She's my teacher," said Ben. "The rooms are down that way although I'm not sure if Patty is still here."

"Thanks."

Felicity adjusted her impractical scarf, picked up her umbrella and made for the door.

"Felicity..." said Ben instinctively as she moved away from him.

She looked back and he could tell she understood his expression perfectly.

"I'll see you in her class next week, yes?" she said.

"Of course," said Ben. "It's rare to meet someone with a similar interest in history."

"Something to discuss over coffee?" she suggested.

He looked down at his still-soaked jumper.

"I'll leave the brolly at home," she said. "Oh. Look."

She bent down and rescued a rectangle of card from under a refectory seat. It was the apple sketch he had made earlier that evening. Felicity passed it to him.

"It's good. Really good," she said and was gone.

Ben lingered over putting the drawing in his folder. He was still alone in the refectory, no sign of Nerys or Clovenhoof, but he no longer cared. He rummaged in his pocket for coins to buy another coffee.

ON THE WAY to the adult education centre the following week, Nerys tried to convince Clovenhoof not to take the Classics class again.

"It's not like you're being paid to do it," she said.

"Then I'll do it for the love," replied Clovenhoof.

"That's not the point," she said. "You're an imposter."

"Oh, really, *Professor* Thomas?"

Nerys grumbled wordlessly.

"Anyway," she said, "where did you learn Latin?"

"Rome," said Clovenhoof as though it was the most obvious of things.

Nerys looked at Ben in the rear view mirror.

"Tell him, Ben. Tell him he can't do it."

Ben had a weird and dreamy look on his face. He had been a bit odd all week and had seemed unusually keen to get to night school that evening. He had even put on a clean T-shirt, a sure sign that strange things were afoot.

"Can't do what?" said Ben.

"Haven't you been listening?"

"No," he said happily.

Nerys scowled.

"What is wrong with you, Ben?"

"Oh, that's easy," said Clovenhoof. "No style. Dead end job. That ugly rash under his-"

"I do not have a dead end job," said Ben. "There's nothing wrong with me. In fact, the complete opposite. I'm just looking forward to tonight's class."

"Yay," said Nerys sarcastically. "More cactuses."

"Cacti," said Clovenhoof.

"Shut up, Latin-boy."

BEN AND NERYS sat down in art class. Ben kept the space next to him free, driving away anyone who tried to take it with excuses and bald-faced rudeness.

Felicity had said she'd be coming. She had to be coming. He had spent many an idle moment over the past week thinking of that smile and those eyes, picturing her standing before him in that long, loopy scarf (and in some of his reveries, not much more), conversation and laughter flowing like a river between them.

As the clock's hands raced to the top of the hour, his eyes fixed on the open doorway with greater ferocity and urgency.

Nerys appeared not to notice, managing to keep up a one-sided conversation about Clovenhoof and his wicked insistence on teaching without pay or qualifications.

"I don't think he actually knows any Latin at all," she said. "I think he just makes it up as he goes along."

The art teacher, Patty, drifted over to the classroom door and, despite Ben's silent prayers and imprecations, closed it. Ben let out an audible whimper.

"Yes, I think he's going to get into a lot of trouble," said Nerys in response.

Patty launched into a gushing description of the class's efforts from last lesson, the evocations of fruit and flora that they had managed to commit to paper. She went on to explain that it was time to take it a step further with a real challenge. Patty gestured to a red leather armchair that she had positioned at the front of the room.

"I thought this was drawing from life," said Ben.

"Well, it used to be a cow," said Nerys. "Maybe next week we'll be drawing a plate of sausages."

"Or some nice chops," suggested Ben.

They both shook their heads, each disappointed in their own way.

The door at the front of the classroom opened and Felicity walked in, wrapped in a white dressing gown.

"Oh!" said Nerys in sudden comprehension.

Ben frowned. He didn't get it. Why had Felicity come like that? Had she forgotten to dress after showering that morning? Did she have one of those psychiatric disorders when people forget the most obvious of things and mistake their wives for hats and whatnot?

That might explain why she had shown an unusual level of interest in him, Ben thought with an almost comforting clarity. Of course the only women interested him would be the mentally ill.

Felicity stepped to the front of the class. She looked round the class, a faint smile of greeting to all. She paused as her gaze met Ben's and her eye twitched in a not-quite wink.

"I don't understand," Ben murmured.

Felicity untied her cord belt, let the dressing gown fall to the floor at her feet and sat back in the armchair. Ben dropped his pencil. It clattered loudly on the floor. He bent to pick it up and considered staying down there, hiding behind the table forever.

Patty was speaking but Ben couldn't hear her over the blood pounding in his ears. He wasn't comfortable with nakedness at the best of times, not even his own. A naked model in the drawing from life class ranked high on his all-time list of embarrassing things to avoid. That the life model was someone he knew, even slightly, made matters worse. That he had entertained some *saucy* thoughts regarding Felicity made this moment unbearably confusing.

Reasoning that he couldn't justify hiding on the floor forever (beside which his calves were already beginning to ache from crouching), he rose slowly. He found that judiciously distancing his face from his sketching board, he could neatly cover Felicity's nakedness, leaving only her head poking above the top of the frame, her small bare feet appearing at the bottom and one hand, on the chair arm to the side.

It was a redundant exercise because, like a man emerging from a dungeon after years of imprisonment and being blinded by the sun, Felicity's body had imprinted itself indelibly on Ben's retina. It was only with an extreme effort of will that he managed to hold his pencil straight.

An hour later, he had drawn something. A hand, two feet and a face. He'd worked on the half-smile diligently and, despite his horror at the overall situation, was not displeased with the results.

Nonetheless, when Patty called a halt to the session and Felicity had covered herself and departed the way she had come in, Ben almost vomited with relief. He packed his materials away hurriedly. For the first time, he looked at Nerys's artistic efforts. Nerys had attacked the paper with dark thick lines, creating something angular, not without interest but somehow cold and loveless.

"What do you think?" she said.

"It's good," he said hurriedly. "Let's go."

"I really struggled to concentrate."

"Mmmm," he agreed. "Let's go."

"Did you notice her nipples pointed in different directions?"

"I really need some fresh air."

"It's like they were cross-eyed. I don't think I could trust a woman with cross-eyed breasts."

Ignoring the gibberish Nerys was spouting, Ben gathered his things and left.

He went to stand on the steps overlooking the car park and found Clovenhoof already there.

"How was Classics?" said Ben without any true enthusiasm or interest.

"Navis volitans mihi anguillis plena est."

"I know what you mean."

"Really? And art class?"

"Oh, don't ask," said Ben, shaking his head. "It was..."

"Hey!" called a friendly voice behind them.

Ben turned.

"Oh, er, hi Felicity," he said.

"I thought I'd missed you in there."

"Yes, er..."

Felicity was fully clothed again but Ben found his gaze unavoidably drawn down, until he was staring at two brass buttons on her double-breasted winter coat.

"I hope I didn't surprise you," she smiled.

"Surprised?" he said in a ridiculously over-nonchalant tone. "Of course not. No, they were lovely. I mean *it* was lovely. The session."

Her smile took on a faintly embarrassed quality.

"And are we still on for a coffee?"

"Coffee?" said Ben. "Yes. Er, now? Or not now? I've got..."

He gestured over his shoulder to indicate the abstract concept of things that needed doing.

"You have?" said Felicity. "That's fine."

"Another time though?" said Ben who, despite the horrors of the evening, wasn't quite prepared to let that rarest of things, an available woman, slip through his fingers. "When I've not got things... you know."

"Sure. Maybe I'll swing by at the end of next week's class."

Ben nodded, not sure or happy about what he was agreeing to.

"That would be..."

"Lovely," said Felicity.

"Lovely indeed."

She gave him a flick of a wave and headed off into the night.

CLOVENHOOF WAS SITTING in front of the television at home when there came a knock at the door.

"Come in," he bellowed. "It's open."

Ben entered the flat.

"Jeremy, can I ask you for your advice?" he said and then stopped. "What are you doing?"

Clovenhoof didn't look up.

"Do you mean what am I doing or what is Nerys doing?" he asked.

Nerys squatted on a pouffe next to the television, an easel before her and a palette of paints in her hand. She had a broad smear of red paint across her forehead.

"I'm doing Jeremy's portrait," she said.

"And I'm watching Eastenders," said Clovenhoof, "and translating it into Latin. Relinquite Ricky, nequam est."

"I think I'll come back later."

"Hey, I thought you wanted my advice."

Clovenhoof watched Ben dither and then stay where he was.

"It's about Felicity."

"Felicity?"

"The girl who asked me out at night school."

"Someone asked you out?" said Nerys, incredulous.

"It was the woman who was our life model in class," explained Ben.

"The naked one?"

"Well, she wasn't naked when she asked me out."

Clovenhoof leaned forward in his chair and looked at Ben.

"You've seen her naked?"

"And that's the problem."

"I have no problem with naked women, Ben. I think chicks should be allowed to get naked whenever they want. I'm no sexist. Shame on you."

"It's just that..." Ben struggled to find the words.

"She has a hideous deformity?" suggested Clovenhoof. "An unsightly mole in the shape of Wales?"

"No," said Ben. "She's beautiful."

Nerys snorted.

"She's got cross-eyed tits."

"She's beautiful," Ben insisted.

"Huh. I don't see what she's got that I haven't."

Clovenhoof shrugged.

"Take your kit off and we'll check."

"I knew you'd be no help," said Ben.

"Whoa, there," said Clovenhoof. "You've been asked out by an attractive young woman who, for some reason, isn't repelled by your nerdy looks or fusty odour but, after having seen her naked, you're having second thoughts because you can now only think of her as a naked woman, not one of those sexless entities you call friends –"

"I hope you're not including me in that," said Nerys.

"- and this nakedness thing is a barrier between you."

Ben stared at him.

"Yes. Yes, that's it. That's exactly what it is."

"I know. This clothed / naked thing is a big fuss over nothing. There's been nothing but trouble ever since you humans discovered it. You know I always believe in getting out the meat and two veg in any social situation."

"Oh, we know," said Nerys.

"It breaks the ice and, in the case of romantic situations, prevents any future disappointment. View before buying, I say."

Ben frowned.

"Are you suggesting that I wave my wang in her face in order to even things up?"

"Yes, I am."

"Great. Thanks for that advice. Nerys?"

Nerys put a hand on her chin thoughtfully, daubing it with a smudge of purple paint.

"You think she's beautiful?"

"Yes, I do," said Ben.

"And me?"

"What?"

She stood up.

"Am I?"

"Was this conversation about you?"

"Oh, so I'm not beautiful."

"I didn't say that. It's all in the eye of the beholder, isn't it?"

"Don't give me that bollocks."

Ben, visibly struggling, rushed forward.

"I mean, look at your painting. Have you painted Jeremy as handsome or..."

"Absolutely bloody handsome," put in Clovenhoof.

Ben stood beside Nerys and looked at her painting.

"That's..."

"What?" she snapped.

"Very good," said Ben honestly.

"You think?"

"You've used a lot of red. He looks a bit sun-burned."

"I know. I'm not sure why I did that."

"And his feet are a bit blocky, almost hoof-like. And what are these two things on his head?"

Nerys made an uncertain noise.

"They just seemed to suit him."

Ben joined in with his own uncertain noise.

"I know what you mean," he said.

Clovenhoof smiled and returned his gaze to the television.

"Egridite domo, lupa!" he said happily.

As they entered the Paradise Adult Education Centre, Ben tried to convince Nerys not to go through with her plan.

"It's not like you're being paid to do it," he said.

"I'm doing it for the love," replied Nerys. "Anyway, it's all arranged with Patty."

"It's obscene."

"Oh, so it's okay for your girlfriend to strip off for the class but ugly Nerys should keep her hideous body under wraps?"

"It's not like that. It's just that it's *you*. It'll be like seeing your mum naked."

Nerys stopped in the corridor and wheeled on Ben.

"I've seen photographs of your mum, Ben."

"Naked ones?" said Clovenhoof.

Nerys scowled at Clovenhoof and then Ben.

"I don't appreciate the comparisons," she said.

"Tell her, Jeremy," Ben pleaded.

Clovenhoof raised his hands.

"I'm just glad that someone is heeding my advice. I'm going to leave you kids to it. Dr Clovenhoof has students waiting."

He walked to his classroom, stopping off on the way as he did each week, to greet the snake in the science lab.

"How's it going?" he said to the snake as he entered.

The snake raised its head.

Clovenhoof patted his pockets for the two dead mice he had brought with him and, after giving an "Ah-ha!" of victory as he found one of them in his wallet, opened the tank and swung the snack by its tail. The serpent struck at the rodent with a speed that never failed to impress Clovenhoof.

"You've no truck with clothes, have you?" he said. "No. Well, what would you wear? A sock?"

"What is that?" whined a voice distantly along the corridor. "Is that body glitter?"

"Humans and this bloody need to hide their wobbly

dangly bits," said Clovenhoof, stroking the snake's scales as it swallowed the mouse. "At least it shows He has a sense of humour."

Clovenhoof glanced up at the clock.

"Class time. Gotta dash."

He nipped across the corridor and into his own classroom.

"Avete, plebes," he said, in greeting, opened his briefcase and piled his text books on his desk. He discovered the second dead mouse inside his hardback copy of Cicero's *On the Republic*. It looked rather pathetic and two-dimensional.

"Ah," he said, wondering if he should keep it for a bookmark. He decided against it and brushed it to the floor.

He turned to the class. Their attentive, loving eyes were fixed on him.

"Right then, class," he said. "Where were we up to last time?"

"We were comparing Roman and Greek texts," said Adrian.

"That's right and we were discussing why Ancient Greek literature was infinitely superior to Roman. Can anyone remember why?"

Odette, she of the unflattering cardigan, put her hand up.

"Odette?"

"Knob jokes," she said.

"That's right. Well done. The Greeks were masters of the knob gag, whereas the average Roman writing was as dry and dull as Western Australia."

"Who are you?"

This question came from the bearded man who had

appeared in the doorway. Clovenhoof thought there was something vaguely familiar about him.

"I'm Dr Clovenhoof. This is my Classics group."

"I'm Dr Wiles. This is *my* Classics group," said the man. "And I've no idea who you are."

Clovenhoof brow furrowed and then realisation dawned.

"Oh, yes. I punched you in the face a couple of weeks ago, didn't I?"

"You?"

"I was attacking my neighbour with an imaginary sword," Clovenhoof explained to the class.

"It *was* you!" exclaimed Dr Wiles.

"Yes, it was. How's the jaw?"

Dr Wiles turned a funny shade of pink.

"How's my jaw? You dislocated it, you delinquent arse. I've spent days in agony. I've had to have two teeth extracted and root canal surgery on a third."

"Ah, well. Aegroto, dum anima est, spes esse dicitur."

"Aegroto...? Come here and-"

Dr Wiles stepped forward, trod on Clovenhoof's squashed mouse and his feet slipped out from under him. He went down onto the floor with a thud and a scream of pain and fury. The class leapt to their feet.

"Is he all right?" asked Odette.

"Are you all right?" Clovenhoof asked Dr Wiles.

Dr Wiles screamed at him again in answer and, though there was still both pain and fury in that scream, the furious aspect had definitely acquired the upper hand.

The classroom door slammed open. Nerys filled the

doorframe, clothed only in a dressing gown and a faint patina of body glitter.

"Nobody touch him!" she commanded. "I'm trained in first aid."

"Aren't you meant to be getting naked next door?" said Clovenhoof.

"I heard his cry and I came," she said melodramatically. "I also wanted to get here ahead of that first aid class in room nine."

She crouched down beside the stricken Dr Wiles.

"Don't worry. I'm here to help."

"Who are you?"

"I'm Nerys. That's all you need to know." She looked up at Clovenhoof. "You'll need to find Ben and get him to tell our teacher that I've been delayed by a mission of mercy."

"Really?"

"Go." She took hold of Dr Wiles's hand. "What appears to be the problem?"

"He slipped on a dead mouse," said Clovenhoof.

Dr Wiles's eyes goggled.

"Are you naked?" he croaked.

Nerys glanced down. Certainly her dressing gown was open more than was properly decent and Dr Wiles possibly had a unique floor-level view. Nerys treated her patient to an angelic smile.

"Yes, I am," she said.

Clovenhoof scuttled across the way and into the art room. The rotund teacher was casting about anxiously whilst trying to deliver some meandering and aimless speech. She looked up at Clovenhoof, clearly hoping to see Nerys.

"A slight technical hitch," said Clovenhoof. He hooked his hand under Ben's elbow and dragged him through the door at the head of the classroom and into the supply cupboard.

"We'll have the show on the road in just a tick," he told the teacher and closed the door.

Ben looked at the neat pile of Nerys's clothes on the one chair in the supply cupboard and the tub of body glitter on top of it. He looked back at Clovenhoof.

"What's going on? Where's Nerys?"

"Bit of an emergency," said Clovenhoof. "She's having to deal with it. You need to step in."

Ben blinked.

"Do what?"

"Step in. Take over."

Ben looked at the pile of clothes again.

"Take over?"

"Yes. Get your clothes off."

Clovenhoof reached for Ben's T-shirt and pulled it up.

"What?" said Ben. "Me? Strip?"

"Exactly. I don't think you need to do the body glitter thing but, yes, strip."

"No, no, no. I can't do this."

"Yes, you can."

Clovenhoof reached for Ben's belt and, with some nifty dexterity, whipped it off him with an audible crack.

"I don't want to do this," said Ben.

"Of course you do. In fact, this is exactly what you want to do."

"How so?"

"You've got those hangs ups about Felicity parading her naughty bits in public. Here's how to redress the balance."

"I'm not sure…"

"Nakedness is nothing to be ashamed of," said Clovenhoof and, to illustrate the point, ripped his own shirt open and let his trousers drop to the floor.

Ben trembled.

"But they're expecting Nerys."

"They're expecting *someone*. You're someone."

There was a rap at the door.

"Is everything all right in there?" called the art teacher.

"Just a minute," replied Clovenhoof. "Almost ready."

"They'll laugh at me," hissed Ben.

"At you?" said Clovenhoof, stepping out of his trousers and shucking off his pants. "But we're beautiful."

"You're coming out with me?"

"I'll be right behind you."

Ben shook his head but unbuttoned his jeans nonetheless.

"I'm going to hate this."

"It'll be cathartic."

"And Nerys needs me to do this?"

"Her exact words."

Ben peeled off his jeans and lifted his T-shirt over his head. Clovenhoof looked at his neighbour, the pale weedy man with ribs like a row of speed bumps.

"Look at you. Just as God intended you to be," said Clovenhoof proudly. Naked, ignorant and compliant he added silently in your head.

Ben nodded affirmatively.

"I'm going to do this," he said.

"Absolutely."

"I'm not ashamed of my body."

"No way."

"I'm happy in my skin."

"Well, no one else would be."

"What?"

ABRUPTLY, a piercing alarm bell began to ring, not just one but several, chorusing and echoing throughout the building.

"Er..." said Ben.

"Oh," said Clovenhoof.

The door opened and Patty, the art teacher, burst in.

"Is there a fire?" said Ben.

The teacher looked down at the two of them and then up.

"Someone's let loose a massive snake!"

Clovenhoof looked down at himself and gave her a modest smile.

"Why thank you for noticing."

The woman looked at him as though he was mad.

"Come on then," she said. "Out!"

"But..." said Ben gesturing to his discarded clothing.

She grabbed his wrist and pulled.

"We have to *evacuate*. The alarm has sounded."

Ben was dragged out into the now empty art room. Clovenhoof followed.

"My pants!" Ben wailed, feeling himself descending into a dream-like state of terror.

"Pants won't save you from a venomous snake," said Patty.

"I don't think pythons are venomous," said Clovenhoof conversationally.

"And how do you know it's a python?" said Ben and suddenly leapt with fright. "It's not here, is it?"

"Out!" commanded Patty.

"I think I might have forgotten to put the lid on the tank," said Clovenhoof.

"Oh, this would be your fault," said Ben witheringly

"Nothing is my fault," Clovenhoof replied.

Pat poked and prodded them down the corridor, past the language labs, the music rooms and pottery studios. Clovenhoof grabbed a couple of items off a nearby trolley.

"Here," he shouted over the noisy alarm. "Cover your *shame.*"

Ben placed the pottery cup over his groin, only just managing to cover the barest of his essentials.

"How come you get a vase?" he said.

Clovenhoof swaggered along with large clay flower vase in his hand.

"Each shall be given according to his needs," he said.

They went out through the fire doors and down into the car park where several dozen people milled in the dark.

"Brrr. Cold out here," said Clovenhoof. "Look, I've got nipples like chapel hat pegs."

Several dozen pairs of eyes had turned to look at the two naked men.

"Oh, God," Ben whimpered. He felt his manhood shrivel up and try to retreat into his body and it was not entirely because of the cold.

Across the way, Nerys, not much better dressed than he, stood with the injured Dr Wiles clinging to her.

And beyond, standing in the faint glow of the streetlights on Paradise Street, was another woman, wrapped up in a thick winter coat and a very long scarf. It was hard to tell at such distant but Ben guessed the expression on her face to be something between confusion and disgust.

"Oh, God," he whimpered again. "I was happy here for a while, Jeremy. And you ruined it."

"That's right. Blame me. Don't blame yourself. Or her."

Felicity stepped backwards, fading into the night.

"To hell with you," snorted Ben angrily.

"Yeah, yeah," said Clovenhoof wearily. "Hey." He elbowed Ben in the ribs and gestured to his vase. "Look. No hands."

2

PATRON SAINT OF NOTHING AT ALL

"St Christopher," said the Archangel. "Do come in. Take a seat."

Christopher gave him a broad grin, nervous around the edges.

"Where would you like me to take it? I can take it anywhere. I can lift anything. Did you know I once carried the infant Christ across a raging river?"

"I believe you've mentioned it once or–"

"Right heavy, he were. Like a lead ball."

"Yes," said the Archangel. "Do just sit. You obviously saw the memo."

"I can't say I rightly understood it," said the huge saint, carefully lowering himself onto the small swivel chair.

"Well." The archangel fiddled briefly with his quill. "First of all, let me say how pleased we all are with you work you've done over the centuries, both on earth and here in the Celestial City. As patron saint of travel and transport you've-"

"And storms."

"And storms."

"And Vilnius, Brunswick and the Island of St Kitts."

"Really? That's very good."

"And toothache."

"What? Sorry?"

"I am the patron saint of toothache and gum ulcers. S'true. You can look it up."

"People with toothache and ulcers pray to you then?"

"Aye," the giant saint nodded modestly. "Bonjella. That were my idea."

The archangel smiled brightly.

"It's quite a career you had."

"Why thank you, Archa-" He stopped. "Had?"

The archangel made a noise.

"Yes, well, you see. As in... let me put it this way. Tell me about your childhood."

"My childhood?"

"Yes. What kind of upbringing you had, what kind of child you were. Where were you born?"

"Born. Yes." Saint Christopher frowned. "I can't quite recall. It were over sixteen hundred years ago."

"Of course. So, tell me something else about your life."

"Anything?"

"Anything."

St Christopher sat in thought for some time.

"Ah," he said, wagging his enormous finger. "There was this one time, after I decided to devote my life to serving the Lord by helping people across this river. Big river. Deep.

Wide. Anyroad, this young child comes up to me and asks me to help him cross."

The archangel nodded.

"Is this the story about when you carried the infant Christ?"

"Have I told you before?"

"You may have done," said the archangel patiently.

"Because, not a lot of people know that my name, Christopher, means 'carrier of Christ.'"

"Ah. And that's the name you were given after your noble deed."

"That's right."

"What did people call you before that?"

"Before they called me Christopher?"

"Mmm. Yes."

St Christopher puffed out his cheeks.

"I... you see, it were a long time ago. It can be hard to remember."

"Your own name?"

"Aye."

The archangel consulted the notes on the table before him.

"You can perhaps see where this is going. Down on earth, the bishop of Rome, his holiness Pope Paul VI has been doing some tidying up of the feast days. He's taken a good long look at your history and he's decided..."

"Yes?"

"He has decided that, um, you didn't exist."

"What?"

"In his *motu proprio Mysterii Paschali*, his holiness has

concluded there is no historical basis to believe you ever existed."

St Christopher was dumbfounded for a good while.

"Bastard!" he finally declared.

"Now, Christopher, please."

"Of course, I exist. Look at me."

"Oh, you exist here and now. Previous popes have declared your existence and, 'as it is on earth so shall it be in heaven,' you are here."

"But now you're getting rid of me?"

"No, dear fellow, we wouldn't be that cruel. We're happy to keep you on. It's just that, officially, technically, you don't exist anymore."

The saint was fuming.

"That little shit never liked me. And he declared it *motu proprio*? That means he just decided it all by himself. He didn't ask anyone else. No committee meetings. No focus groups. One man. Who the fuck does he think he is?"

The archangel clasped his hands together and leaned forward.

"He's the pope, Christopher. He's God's representative on earth."

"He's a tit. That's what he is."

"You really mustn't take this personally," said the archangel. "Many saints have been deleted."

"Deleted!" squeaked St Christopher.

"He's removed Telephorus, Hyginus –"

"Well, they're *clearly* made up saints."

"- Felix, Marcellus, Canute, Emerentina, Valentine –"

"St Valentine?"

"Yes. Gone."

"I can't believe it."

"I think many of us were thinking the whole Valentine's day thing was getting too tacky anyway."

"But Valentine. He's a mate of mine."

"And will remain so."

"We used to go do them Caribbean love cruises. He'd stoke up the fires of romance. I'd stop the boat sinking."

"And we appreciate what you did but it stops now," said the archangel.

"All of it?"

"Your status as saint has been... revoked. You cannot intercede on God's behalf."

"But when people pray to me..."

"They can't."

"Oh, I see," said the indignant saint. "So who's going to help people with their transport issues now?"

"Apparently, there's something called SatNav that the boys in the lab are working on right now."

"But who, do tell, will be fighting the good fight against my opposite number?"

"Opposite number?"

"Stinkybus. Patron demon of traffic jams, lost luggage and public transport."

"I am sure we will be able to put something in place," the archangel assured him.

St Christopher shook his head miserably.

"He never forgave me."

"Who?"

"Pope Paul VI."

"This isn't personal."

"Isn't it? Isn't it? Northern Italy, 1919. His bloody holiness, before he was even ordained, was on a cycling holiday. He was wearing his St Christopher medallion and I fulfilled my duties to him. I had watched over him the entire holiday. I made sure his trains were on time. I diverted the black clouds that threatened to ruin his day. I did everything. You hear me?"

"I do. I do," said the archangel.

"I am the patron saint of travel, aren't I? Am I the patron saint of bloody shoddy necklaces? Am I?"

"No?" said the archangel.

"No," said St Christopher. "It weren't my fault. While he was cycling along the shore, the chain on his medallion broke. Down it went, medallion and chain, right into his gears. Locked the wheels and threw them into Lake Garda."

"Oh dear."

"Oh dear, indeed. His girlfriend wasn't impressed either."

"Did she see it happen?"

"She was sat on the handlebars."

The archangel considered this at length.

"Unfortunate."

"Unlucky," said St Christopher. "And that git's had it in for me ever since. I wouldn't even put it past him to go for the papacy just so he could do this to me."

"I think that's a bit far-fetched, Christopher."

"Is it? Shifty bugger, that one." He sighed. "So, is that it, then?"

The archangel closed the file in front of him.

"Pretty much."

The saint shrugged.

"And what do I do with my time now?"

"We'd like you to take up a post at the Non-Specific Prayer Assessment Unit."

St Christopher pulled a face.

"The 'OhGodohGodhelpme' helpline?"

"It's vital work, Christopher. Any plea to the Almighty must be heard."

"You're going to put me in a call centre?"

"It's not that bad," said the archangel smoothly. "It's housed in a nice new building over by the Jehovah's Witness ghetto. Will you be able to find your way there all right?"

The former patron saint of travel shot him a filthy look and then, before the archangel had a chance to move, punched him in the gob with his mighty fist.

The archangel fell to his knees, clutching his mouth.

"'otally uncalled for," he moaned. "You've knocked my 'ucking 'ooth out. Really 'urts."

"Oh, you know what you can do about that then, don't you?" said Christopher and gave him the finger and left.

3

CLOVENHOOF AND THE SNOWMEN

Clovenhoof looked out of his kitchen window and down at the snow-covered garden.

"Oh," he said in sudden understanding.

Life on earth among the mortal human scum was a constant education. All the little rules of human behaviour.

For instance, if someone says 'Love me, love my dog,' it's not to be taken as an invitation.

For instance, if you run out of toilet paper, it's not socially acceptable to use the curtains.

And, for instance, some things on television look like they're made up but are actually real and some things look real but are made up.

Clovenhoof ran through his little mental check-list.

Eastenders was NOT a fly-on-the-wall documentary.

24 hours in A&E WAS a fly-on-the-wall documentary and not a sitcom.

David Cameron and Nick Clegg were NOT a ventriloquist act.

And, thought Clovenhoof, mentally adding it to his list, Raymond Brigg's *The Snowman* was NOT a whimsical cartoon but a public safety information film about the dangers of building a zombie snowman in your own back garden.

For there was the evidence shambling right before Clovenhoof's eyes, opening the garden gate with its snowy paws and stumbling out into the lane. The snowman that he'd built with Ben had come to life!

"What have I done?" he gasped.

He had wondered why there wasn't more of an outcry from the parents in *The Snowman* when the snowman came alive, abducted their son and flew off with him. But there was definitely going to be an outcry over this.

There were zombie snowmen stalking the streets of Boldmere. Did other people know about this? Would they blame him? He'd only just finished serving the community service order following that unfortunate business at the church nativity. It would be prison this time!

And, he reminded himself, *Busty Prison Babes 9* was NOT a documentary.

If the zombie snowmen were real, could they be stopped? And wasn't he too much of a coward to be a zombie-defeating hero?

"No," he growled, slapping his fist into his hand. "They *must* be stopped."

Of course he would save the day. He'd held his own in

celestial battles hadn't he? He might be a bit rusty, but how agile could an undead snowman really be?

He did a few practice lunges in his lounge to be sure. It felt good to be preparing for action.

He'd need weapons. He went to the cupboard of useful things and grabbed a selection.

By the time he'd clanked to the bottom of the stairs with his armoury, he realized that he needed a steed to carry him into battle. He didn't think he'd find a horse in Boldmere, but Mrs Galloon's mobility scooter was parked outside her house two doors down. He was certain that she'd approve of her scooter being used for such a selfless and necessary endeavor, so stowed his weaponry in the basket and set off down the road.

He quickly realized the problem was worse than he'd anticipated. A thick blanket of snow had proven irresistible to the local children and they'd been out in force, building snowmen.

"Fools!" he hissed dramatically. "When will man ever learn?"

There was no sign of the shambler that had escaped from his own garden but several stood in their unawoken state in front gardens. He was able to dispatch several as he drove by, decapitating them with wild swings of a golf club. However, this approach came to an abrupt end when the golf club got wedged in the chest of a large snow-zombie and the damnable creature pulled Clovenhoof from his seat.

The scooter swerved into a garden wall and stalled. Clovenhoof went into a combat roll and came to his feet with a dustbuster in his hand.

"Ha!" he declared, thrusting his weapon at the gargantuan enemy. He pressed the button and it whined into life. He'd been impressed to discover that it would suck up solids or liquids, so he was certain that it would work on snow.

He drove it into the snowman's face grunting and shouting with battle-rage as he gouged its features.

The dustbuster quickly filled with snow and Clovenhoof realized that he hadn't reduced the snowman by more than a tiny fraction. He started using it as a club instead, battering the snowman and scattering the decomposing contents of the dustbuster as it splintered into pieces. He tossed the remains over his shoulder as he moved away, satisfied that he'd disabled this particularly fearsome snowman.

He then spotted, across the way, a large garden in which a pair of youngsters were surrounded by not one but four of the monsters. The kids, stumbling around in their bulky coats and mittens, were either unaware of the danger they were in or had been driven senseless by fear. Yes, that must be it.

Clovenhoof leapt aboard the scooter and zipped across the road with a cry of "Fear not, little ones!"

He delved into the scooter basket and pulled out the flamethrower. Clovenhoof kept a flamethrower for cooking, putting the finishing touches to crème brulees and such. He'd stolen it from a council road crew and it could be a little overpowered for culinary use, but he was confident it was just the thing for zombie snowmen.

He ignited the flame and it roared into life. He hurdled the wall, took up a manly pose and doused the nearest snowman in flame. It melted soundlessly, with just the occasional pop from a twig that was rolled up in the snow.

By this time, the children had thankfully realised the seriousness of their position and had begun screaming.

"Run!" Clovenhoof yelled. "Save yourselves."

He blasted the second snowman but then as he leaned in to reduce the third snowman to nothing the flame sputtered and died.

He shook the flame thrower. It felt light.

"Out of fuel!" he cursed and turned to find the fourth snowman right behind him. Trying to sneak up on him! It was a small one, but it sported a hat, similar to the one in the cartoon. Perhaps a symbol of rank.

Fear and powerful devilish reflexes kicked in. Clovenhoof drove a fist into the snowman's face and then gave it a kick in the snowballs. The beast crumbled in silent agony.

He leapt over the wall again and, as he mounted his scooter, he saw a gathering group of people watching him from down the road. Clovenhoof smiled at the grateful on-lookers.

Further on there were three more snowmen close together. Clovenhoof knew that he needed yet more extreme disposal methods for this combined threat.

He smiled smugly, knowing that keeping the leftover fireworks from Bonfire Night had been the right thing to do, whatever Nerys and Ben had said to him. He made a pile in the centre of the snowmen, glancing up frequently, to be sure that they weren't coming to life and slipping away while he was concentrating.

He lit the fuse and then moved away on the scooter.

The first firework was colourful but not destructive. It illuminated the scene with a fine spray of pink and purple sparks, but left the snowmen intact. Things got much more interesting when the rockets started going off. Clovenhoof was impressed to see a head blown completely off. The next one embedded itself in the side of a snowman and made a frustrated whizzing sound while going nowhere. The last of the big rockets shot between the snowmen and went over the heads of the crowd up the street.

Clovenhoof frowned. The fireworks hadn't been quite as useful as he'd pictured for destroying the snowmen. He needed to finish the job himself. He reached into the basket and brought out a cricket bat. He took a run up at the snowmen and started swinging. He shrieked and bellowed as he battered the snowmen, losing himself in the frenzy of the battle against these terrible creatures.

When he'd flattened all three, he realized that the crowd was approaching, and that the people from inside the house were also coming out.

"Yes, I've called the police. I told them he's armed-"

Clovenhoof beamed at them.

"You don't have to thank me. I've saved you all. You can go back inside now."

He turned around and saw that there was a crowd on the other side as well.

"Well it's lovely to see you all, but I'm going to slip away now, like superheroes do."

A couple of large men stepped forward in a manner that was not friendly.

The smile fell from Clovenhoof's lips as he understood in

an instant that these people were hostile. He hefted the cricket bat in his hands and wondered if he could break through the line and make a run for it.

At that moment a car drew up.

"Get in!" yelled Nerys.

Clovenhoof moved swiftly and was buckled in and speeding away seconds later.

"WHAT WERE YOU THINKING?" yelled Nerys. "Mrs Galloon saw you take her scooter so I knew you were doing something ridiculous, but *this*?"

"I was saving you all! How can I be the only one to see that there's a supernatural menace stalking the streets of Boldmere!"

"What are you babbling about?"

"Zombie snowmen. Like they had on the telly. I thought that cartoon was a work of fiction."

"The Snowman? Of course it's fiction, you idiot," yelled Nerys.

"Well I saw one come to life. Walking out of our garden this morning. How do you explain that?"

Nerys drove on, lips clamped in a straight line.

"There was a snowman in our garden?"

"Yeah, Ben and I had been building one. We'd made a massive ball for the body, huge it was. The trouble was, we'd used all of the snow in the garden, and we needed some more to make the head. I went upstairs and opened the skylight and pushed the snow off the roof with a broom."

"Right," said Nerys. "I bet it all fell down in one big go, didn't it?"

"Yeah!" said Clovenhoof. "It made a brilliant kind of a *whump* noise when it did."

Nerys pulled up outside the flats.

"Was Ben out in the garden when you did this?"

Clovenhoof paused in the act of getting out of the car, a stricken look on his face. "Oh no, so you think the zombie snowman got him!"

"Jeremy," said Nerys. "I think I know-"

She stopped. Clovenhoof turned. The snowman raised his arms to grab Clovenhoof.

"Wait!" said Nerys but Clovenhoof had the bat in his hand and had already clonked the menace on the side of the head. It went down with a thud.

Clovenhoof raised the bat for the *coup de grace*.

"It's Ben!" yelled Nerys.

Clovenhoof hesitated.

"What? Oh."

Clovenhoof groaned in understanding as Ben groaned with pain.

"I get it now," he said. "He was just pinching my snow so he could make his own snowman. How terribly irresponsible."

4

SAINT NICHOLAS AND THE KRAMPUS

"Have you seen *Home Alone*?"

"No."

"No?"

"No."

"What about *Home Alone 2: Lost in New York*?"

"No," said St Nicholas. "I have not seen it."

"Really?" said Joan of Arc, swishing her sword at the mist around their ankles. "It's a classic."

"Is it?"

"In this one, Kevin McAllister accidentally gets on the wrong plane and has to spend Christmas alone in a swish New York hotel while trying to foil the plans of the burglars he tangled with in the first film."

"I see," said St Nicholas, squinting to peer through the hazy fog of Limbo. "And this is a Christmas movie?"

"Yes."

"What makes it a Christmas movie?" he asked.

"Well," said the teenage saint. "It takes place at Christmas time."

"Yes?"

"And nothing says Christmas like a twelve year old smacking grown men in the face with paint pots and bags full of hammers."

The bald and long-bearded saint made a noise in his throat.

"I don't really think it's helping your case," he said.

"I'm just saying that Christmas is a lot of fun, Nick. I mean, I'm really grateful you chose to come along today but there's so much more to Christmas."

"There are the praises offered to our Lord and the holy communion taken in his name," said St Nicholas. "That is Christmas."

"Well, yes," said Joan, "but there is the other stuff as well. The songs, the feasts, the nativity plays –"

"I don't object to the plays," said St Nicholas.

"- and then, on that magical night, all the children go to bed early, even though they're too excited to sleep, and wait for that moment when the sleigh comes and Sa-"

"Don't!" snapped St Nicholas.

"I'm just saying."

"I know. I don't like that name. Or any of the names. I am not that fat horrible pagan spirit."

"You're not fat," said Joan.

"No, that's not my point."

"Although you have a lovely white beard and red really suits you."

"Joan. I am many things. I am a symbol of charity. I did

indeed devote my life to gift giving and helping the less fortunate. I am the patron saint of children, archers, thieves –"

"Did not know that."

"– as well as the patron saint of moneylenders and pawnbrokers –"

"Well, that is very Christmassy."

" – but I am not him. Is that clear?"

"As crystal," said Joan. "Sorry. I'm just glad you agreed to come with me."

"You're welcome."

Joan looked up but there was no sun or moon in this no man's land, just an all-encompassing greyness that swirled around them, above and below. The Celestial City was a long way behind them.

"The Krampus is late," she said.

"Of course he is," said St Nicholas. "I remember this place when it was full of unbaptised children."

"Oh, yeah," said Joan nodding in recollection. "What happened to them?"

"The amnesty. They've all been transferred to the Swedenborg crèches. Never had children myself."

"No, me neither."

"I do like them though."

"You rescued three lads from a butcher once, didn't you?" she said.

"That's right. *That* was me. 323AD."

"I forget. He was going to chop them up and sell them off as ham or something?"

The saint shook his head.

"He'd already done the foul deed. Killed them, butchered their bodies and left the bits in a barrel to cure."

"And this story has a happy ending?" said Joan, a look of concern on her face.

"I prayed over their remains and, by the Almighty's power, the little lads leapt out, whole and healthy."

"And screaming, I should imagine."

"They were remarkably sanguine about the entire thing," said St Nicholas.

"That's pretty impressive, Nick."

"A bit showy in my own opinion. One does not need miracles to do the Lord's work. My best work was the giving of gifts of gold to three unmarried daughters. You know that one?"

"Think so," said Joan. "The father was too poor to pay dowries to any man so they were destined to become prostitutes."

"That's right. So, on three successive nights, I threw a bag of gold coins in through the man's window. One bag for each daughter. Except, on the third night he was expecting me and was looking out of the window, so I had to climb onto the roof and drop it down the chimney."

"Oh, I see! Just like Sa-"

"Don't! I told you."

"Sorry. It was good work. A great example to the faithful and you saved those women from a life of wickedness."

St Nicholas coughed uncomfortably.

"You did stop them becoming prostitutes, didn't you?" she asked.

He grimaced.

"I stopped them becoming poor prostitutes," he said.

"Oh, well, you tried," said Joan brightly and then suddenly stiffened. "Do you hear that?"

"I can *smell* that," said St Nicholas. "It's him."

There was the muffled yet echoing clip-clop of hooves on rock and a foetid stench: rank and animalistic but with a foul sulphurous edge. It smelled like a wet sheep rolled in rotten eggs.

The Krampus stepped out of the mist, a smaller demon carrying a huge sack at its side.

"Put it down there, Rutspud," rasped the Krampus, struggling to articulate around its enormous tongue.

"Yes, sir," said the demon obediently.

The Krampus was an eight-foot tall goat man but that simple description could not hope to encapsulate the utter nastiness of this demon. From his yellow eyes to his yellow fangs, from his long questing tongue to the clanking chains that hung from his arms, the Krampus was a deliberate affront to everything that was pleasant and cosy and safe. Joan was amazed that people used to let this thing into their homes on Christmas Eve...

"You're late, Krampus," said Joan and realised her grip on her sword had tightened.

"Tough titties, Joan," said the Krampus. "Long time no see, Santa."

"You don't know me," said St Nicholas in restrained irritation.

"Sure I do. Europe. The Middle Ages. We were the greatest double act since Samson and Delilah."

"Double act?" spat St Nicholas.

"Come on, Santa," said the Krampus and then turned to his demon underling. "You should have seen us, Rutspud. Rat-a-tat-tat on the door on a winter's night. In we'd go. Santa here would give presents to all the nice kiddy-winks and I would stuff all the naughty ones in my basket. Lots of naughty children."

"It must have been a big basket, sir," said Rutspud.

"No. Not at all," said the Krampus. "But I do have big powerful hands."

St Nicholas shook his head in disgust.

"Please, Joan, let us get this over with."

Joan pulled a scroll from within the plates of her armour and unrolled it.

"According to the terms of the Inferno-Celestial Accord of two thousand and ten," she read, "we are here to exchange Christmas care packages. One sack to be given from Heaven to Hell and one sack of equal size and weight from Hell to Heaven."

The Krampus grabbed the neck of Hell's sack and thrust it out. Warily, St Nicholas picked up Heaven's sack and stepped forward to meet him. The lofty saint and the shaggy demon eyed each other for a long second and then passed their burdens over. St Nicholas closed his eyes as he assessed the weight of Hell's offering. The Krampus licked his own eyeball and jiggled Heaven's gift thoughtfully.

"Close enough," said St Nicholas sourly.

"It'll do," conceded the Krampus. "No books of scripture this time?"

"No curses or hexes?" replied Joan.

"Them's the rules," said the Krampus with a grin. "You know, shiny tits, I look forward to this every year. You have no idea how grateful I am."

"Glad to provide you with some amusement," she said with a forced smile.

This whole Christmas present venture had indeed been Joan's idea. It had started as a simple notion, to get the residents of the Celestial City to send cards and letters of consolation and love to the damned of Hell at that most special time of year. It was a simple plan and one with only two barriers, to wit, Heaven and Hell.

Heaven might have been the realm of charity and forgiveness. However, it also had a stranglehold on righteousness and sermonising and the first batch of cards that came in response to Joan's appeal to the blessed faithful had more than an ounce of snobbery, disdain and schadenfreude about them. Joan had to send most of them back and most of the second wave too, and the third... until she was compelled to provide a set of strict guidelines for submissions.

Hell's problem, naturally, was that they had no interest in accepting anything that might make the plight of the damned any less wretched. What was in it for them? Of course, if Hell could reciprocate, exchanging the consoling gifts of Heaven for the disturbing gifts of Hell then that would be another matter entirely. The enterprise then became one of bargaining, ensuring that the gifts were of equal value, weight for weight, happiness for grief, comfort and joy for discomfort and misery. Heaven's gifts were destined for the most wretched of the damned. Hell's gifts were delivered to members of the blessed dead who signed up to the scheme for the sake of others.

There had been mistakes in the those early exchanges. Icons, relics and works of scripture, both holy and diabolical were simply a no-no. Like matter and anti-matter, they simply could not exist in the opposing realm. There had been explosions, generally deemed horrific by Heaven and not horrific enough by Hell. It also transpired that while Heaven ran on alternating current for its electricity supplies, Hell had taken up with direct current. That had proved disappointing in the year that Heaven sent all those fridge freezers in exchange for Hell's karaoke machines.

The Krampus opened Heaven's sack and removed a sample present. He snipped away the silver bow with a razor-sharp claw.

"Let's see what shite you've given us this year. Ah, the usual. Water. Bandages. Prescription painkillers. Oh, look. *The Little Book of Calm*."

"You should read it," said St Nicholas, hesitating in opening one of Hell's packages. It was wrapped in blood-spattered newspaper and tied with what might have been a length of intestine.

"You really want to open *that* one?" said the Krampus.

"Something to hide?" said St Nicholas with false bravado and peered inside.

He regarded the contents critically.

"The old favourites. A parasitic wasp. Ebola flavoured

chocolate. A Richard Dawkins book. And a fresh human stool."

"The traditional Christmas turd," agreed the Krampus.

"And what's this?"

St Nicholas pulled out a square sided box covered with an arrangement of coloured tiles.

"A Rubik's Cube," said the Krampus. "It's a puzzle."

"And it explodes when you complete it?"

"No."

"It's covered in contact poison?"

"Nope."

"Well, that doesn't seem particularly evil."

"I know. That's the beauty of it."

"So, are we happy?" asked Joan.

"Hell is never happy," muttered the demon, Rutspud.

Krampus shrugged and deftly resealed the present.

"Oh, you've dropped something," said Joan, pointing to a small rectangle of paper drifting down from the Krampus's hand.

The beastly demon snatched it out of the air.

"What is it?" he growled, tongue flicking.

"We're putting them in every package this year," said Joan.

The Krampus held it at arm's length to read the small writing.

"Question: Why is a Christmas tree like a Roman Catholic Priest?" He frowned. "Answer: They both have ornamental balls."

Rutspud sniggered. The Krampus re-read the joke, his

goaty lips mouthing silently, and then gave a low, throaty laugh.

"Good one," he said, "I'll have to tell the boys that."

Joan gave St Nicholas an arch look.

"Told you they'd like the Christmas cracker jokes," she said.

The Krampus flung the parcel back in the sack and tossed it to Rutspud.

"Until next year. Santa. Joan."

The Krampus strode off in the general direction of Hell, with his minion tottering in his wake. There was a chuckle from the mists.

"Balls," the Krampus laughed to himself, and was gone.

St Nicholas retied the ribbon of gut, put the present back in the sack and hoisted the whole thing onto his shoulder.

"I can't stand that creature," he said.

"It's done now," said Joan. "And we've given Hell a few laughs. A masterstroke even though I do say so myself."

Joan led the way through the mists of Limbo towards the Celestial City.

"So, tell me. Back in the day, did you and the Krampus really do that?"

"What?" said St Nicholas.

"The old good cop, bad cop routine. Carrot and stick."

St Nicholas sniffed haughtily.

"Times were different then."

"You did do it!"

"You can't judge me by modern standards."

"Hey, I'm not judging."

St Nicholas sighed.

"Sorry, I didn't mean to offend you," she said.

"It's not that," he said. "It's that joke. Ornamental balls?"

"What about it?"

"I don't get it," said St Nicholas.

Joan smiled.

"Nope. Me neither. Heaven's this way."

5

DETRITUS AT THE CHURCH FETE

Detritus patted down the pockets of the clothes he was wearing. It appeared that he was undercover. His outfit was rather bland. Brown canvas trousers and a plain cotton shirt. He wondered briefly if he was to be on demon duty at Marks and Spencer, making sure that the clothes were hung on hangers declaring the wrong size and mixing up the pairs of shoes. That was a sought-after gig, nice and easy. He glanced at his right hand. At least he had a pitchfork. One of the modern, folding types. Sweet.

He found a card in one of his pockets. He sighed. This was new.

Demon: Detritus

Mission: Your goal is to disrupt the fund raising efforts of individual churches, and make sure they can't afford to refurbish the buildings.

Stretch goal: Causing misery amongst parishioners as you achieve your main goal.

Special power: You cannot lose at Tombola.

Detritus raised an eyebrow at his special power. He had no idea what Tombola was. He would need to look that up.

TWO DAYS later he strolled onto the vicarage lawn at St Oswalds. It was a beautiful day. Why couldn't he have a special power to disrupt the weather? That would be the fastest way to de-rail a church fete. Never mind, he would make sure that this fete made no money at all. Ideally he would see them make a loss!

Events were just getting started. Stalls lined the lawn, and in the centre was a roped-off area to be used for events. A large marquee labelled *beer tent* was already proving popular, and another marquee held displays of garden produce and baking for judging later on. There was a children's play area, and Detritus decided to start there. A quick flick of his pitchfork and the bouncy castle sagged and deflated. He repeated the same manoeuvre to take out the paddling pool on the hook-a-duck stall. As the side wall collapsed, the water flowed over the top and the ducks bobbed briefly on a small river and came to rest on the grass. He would come back in a minute and plaster candy floss onto some of the table-top games.

He decided to test his special power. He'd researched Tombola, and it was a straightforward game of chance. You would buy one or more tickets from a mixed-up barrel, and if your ticket matched a labelled up prize, then it was yours. He had seen much debate on the subject. There was an implied rule that said you would have a one in ten chance of winning if "all tickets ending in a zero were winners" but of course, there was nothing at all to stop the unscrupulous and underhand practice of adding extra tickets ending in the other digits. He had nodded in approval at that. Sowing the seeds of suspicion and mistrust? Some demon had done well to invent this fiendish game.

There were multiple tombolas. He started at the general tombola and queued behind some eager children who were murmuring to each other in admiration at the top prizes of large stuffed animals. The four who were ahead of him were disappointed to win nothing. When it was his turn he bought ten tickets. He unwrapped each one to reveal a ticket ending in zero. The first three made the lady behind the stall chuckle with admiration. After that she started double-checking the serial numbers on the tickets and sighing theatrically.

"Would you like a carrier bag?" she asked.

He nodded, and wondered how big a carrier bag she might have, as he had won three stuffed toys which were each the size of a Labrador. She wordlessly handed him a tiny, ripped carrier bag and turned her attention to the next customer.

He dragged his haul across the grass to where he saw a wheelbarrow. He loaded up, but before he moved on to the next tombola he made a quick diversion into the adjacent garden where he'd previously spotted a wasps' nest in the back of a privet hedge. He gave it a vigorous poke with his pitchfork, breaking the nest apart, then he scampered away back to the fete. The marquee with the baking was still fairly quiet, so he was able to access the jam display without attracting attention. Once there was a good, thick coating of jam around the back of each table he returned to his wheelbarrow and moved on to the bottle tombola. He bought enough tickets to ensure that no prizes remained and loaded up the wheelbarrow with his winnings.

A small girl appeared at his side.

"I'm Annabel. Can I have the teddy please?" she lisped.

"No," Detritus replied.

"What are you going to do with all of those toys?" asked Annabel. "My mommy says that the Christian thing to do is to share our things."

"Your mommy might be right," said Detritus. "Which is why I'm keeping them all."

"You're a demon aren't you?" said Annabel.

Detritus whirled to face her.

"What?" he hissed. "Of course not. Why would you think that?"

"I saw you using your pitchfork," she said, "and you look like a demon."

"Everyone knows that children have over-active imaginations, so don't bother trying to tell any grown-ups," said Detritus. "Now scram. I've got work to do."

She ran across the lawn to join a group of children, glancing back once or twice. The dog show was about to begin. There was some disruption caused by a sudden swarm of wasps, but the dog owners were battling on and trotted around the circuit with their animals.

Detritus took the ultrasonic dog trainer from his pocket and pressed the button. The dogs reacted instantly. Some of them dropped to the ground and whined while others jerked free of their owners and ran towards Detritus. He walked briskly towards the produce marquee, opening a fresh packet of dog treats as he went.

He targetted a red setter with a clearly boisterous nature, and waved a treat at it.

"Come on then! You can have this if you're good."

He waited until the dog was focussed on the treat and then tossed it onto the table with the cakes. He repeated the same technique with some other dogs, throwing handfuls of treats as they caught on to the game. They leaped and scrambled in amongst the cakes, tipping them off display stands and skidding through the remains.

A border collie started to dig a hole in the lawn, spraying soil into the mix as he pedalled frantically.

Detritus melted away as owners caught up with dogs and tried to drag them away from the giant cakey mess, but the dogs were lapping eagerly at chocolate, icing and cream. A spaniel rolled in the remains of a victoria sponge and then jumped up at all the running humans, thinking it was a huge game.

The wasps had started to cluster around the area, and were soon homing in on human and canine targets who were liberally coated with tempting sugar.

Howls went up from the victims of wasp stings, and the flailing, flapping mob of dog owners spilled out onto the lawn, dogs jumping up and knocking them over with excitement.

Detritus sighed with pleasure at the sight before him. He reached for his bag and grabbed a handful of leaflets that he'd created. They were a modification of a standard leaflet from an ambulance-chasing solicitor. This new leaflet was aimed at a much more niche market.

Been injured or humiliated at a Church Fete? it asked.

It went on to explain that large amounts of compensation might be won from one of the richest organisations in Britain. He considered it a master stroke. No time to bask in glory yet, though, he had work to do. He dropped a leaflet into every handbag or pocket he could access. He made sure that he left a batch at every point that people might pass on their way out, assuming they weren't distracted by wasp stings or hyped up dogs snapping at their ankles.

"Can I have the teddy now?"

Detritus scowled when he saw that Annabel had reappeared.

"Didn't I already say no? Why would I have changed my mind?"

"Because I saw you spoil the dog show," she said, staring up at him, "and I'm going to tell my mommy."

"Tell your mommy if you like. I'm going now, my work here is done," said Detritus, smugly.

"Don't you want to see how far down that dog can get?" asked Annabel.

"What dog?"

"That one there, that's digging the hole. That's the one that was going to win the dog show. I saw it in the rehearsal and it can do somersaults."

Detritus rolled his eyes but he moved forward, curious.

"Look after the wheelbarrow and you can have the teddy," he told Annabel.

The collie was around five feet below the surface of the

lawn and was still digging. A sizeable arc of soil surrounded the hole, and the remains of the crowd who hadn't been stung by wasps or chased by cake-splattered dogs surrounded the hole at a safe distance to watch in curiosity. The church warden, a tall, skinny man wearing a t-shirt emblazoned "Cowboy of Faith" made a couple of moves to catch the dog, but its superior agility made him stumble into the hole instead.

Detritus pushed forward through the crowd, keen to enjoy the moment.

"Are you all right, Peter?" called a woman nearby, peering anxiously into the hole.

Peter pushed himself up onto his elbows and nodded.

"I'm fine. We need to control these dogs, I'd better call the dog warden."

It seemed to Detritus that the collie turned to Peter and gave him a look. It took his sleeve between its teeth and tugged him towards the centre of the hole.

"Oh! Oh! It's attacking me! Someone help – wait, what's this?" Peter crawled to the deepest part of the hole and scraped soil away from something solid. The collie stood back and watched as Peter moved more soil with his hands. After a few minutes, someone handed him a spade and he exposed a flat surface the size of a lap tray. Half an hour later, he hauled a wooden chest out of the hole onto the grass.

"I think I need an expert to open this, it might be an antique," said Peter, grasping the handle on the front of the ancient chest to drag it forward. There was a collective groan of disappointment from the crowd at this anti-climax.

Detritus turned away, but then he whirled back as Peter

yelled out in pain. The handle had pulled clean off the chest, which had fallen onto his foot and collapsed.

The unmistakeable gleam of gold made the crowd gasp. Dozens of coins, and some ornate candlesticks tumbled across the grass.

Detritus shook his head in disbelief. He glanced across at the collie, who was looking directly at him, tongue lolling out in what looked like laughter.

He stomped back to get his wheelbarrow full of booty, but it wasn't there. He saw Annabel surrounded by children who were squealing with excitement as they pulled the giant soft toys out and made off with them, smiling and laughing.

It was all too much. Detritus had to get out of there. A pleasing calamity had been completely ruined with optimism, smiles and laughter.

A WEEK LATER, Detritus was toasting bread on his pitchfork and reading the local paper. He growled with impotent rage when he found the write-up of the church fete.

Church's future secured by discovery of ancient treasure.

Parishioners at St Oswalds church could not believe their luck when they unearthed a priceless hoard of gold at their summer fete.

One of many fundraising activities organised by the cash-strapped parish in an effort to repair the roof, the fete took an unusual turn when several dogs started to behave in a rather eccentric manner. A border collie single-pawdedly dug up nearly a quarter of a ton of soil in exactly the right spot to reveal the hidden treasure.

Thought to have been hidden in an effort to protect the church's riches from the agents of Henry VIII the gold has remained hidden since the sixteenth century. The collie, who has been hailed a "hero" and a "miracle" by locals has vanished. Parishioners have offered a reward to the owner, but so far nobody has come forward.

In the final twist of the day, a mysterious benefactor who enjoyed a winning streak on the fete's tombola stalls made sure that all of the children in attendance left with smiles on their faces as he gave out the toys and gifts that he had won and then disappeared as mysteriously as the dog.

6

CLOVENHOOF AND THE SPIDERS

Nerys came downstairs to find Clovenhoof breaking down a large cardboard box by the front door of the flats.

"I always wonder what you're up to when I see you get parcels in the mail," she said. "Hopefully it's just an inflatable woman, and not something that will explode or set fire to the house."

"Actually," said Clovenhoof, standing up, "I am undertaking an entirely selfless exercise. This little project of mine is to help Ben. Furthermore, it was based on *your* idea."

"Well, how nice," said Nerys. "So what exactly are you doing?"

Clovenhoof beamed.

"Do you remember the other night when we were in the pub?"

"We're in the pub every night."

"The night Ben hurt his elbow."

.   .   .

BEN HAD SEEMED to be in genuine pain. Gasping as he struggled to lift his pint of cider.

"What's wrong with you?" Nerys had asked.

"Tennis elbow," he winced.

"I knew a man who had golf balls," said Clovenhoof, sipping his Lambrini.

"You don't play tennis," said Nerys.

"Some of those books in my shop are quite heavy, I'll have you know." Ben gave a sudden shriek, leapt up onto his seat and pointed. "What was that?"

Clovenhoof and Nerys swiveled their heads to peer at the corner of the pub.

Clovenhoof walked over and picked up a spider, which raced across his hands.

"Kill it!" squealed Ben.

Clovenhoof rolled his eyes and walked to the door, where he shook it outside.

"You're not really that scared of such a small thing are you?" Nerys asked.

Ben took a hearty swig of his drink and then whimpered at his tennis elbow.

"Always have been," he said. "Too many legs. Way they move. Urgh."

"I was reading a magazine article about people who've been cured of their phobias," said Nerys. "They sent someone on a "tarantula experience", and he realised there was nothing to be scared of."

Ben gave her a withering look.

"That sounds like torture."

"It's quite clever," said Clovenhoof. "I like it."

He had long ago ceased to be amazed by the fact that any Hellish torture his demons could devise had already been devised, tried and improved by human beings. Guantanamo Bay, I'm a Celebrity, Weight Watchers...

"It's stupid," said Ben. "I bet that was in America or Essex or somewhere. Luckily nobody round here is about to try anything so ridiculous."

AT THE FLATS, Nerys dropped her keys and her face drained of blood as she stared at the *empty* box in Clovenhoof's hands.

"You haven't?" she whispered.

Clovenhoof nodded, with a wide grin.

"I have just set up the ultimate tarantula experience for Ben. Did you know that *anyone* can buy tarantulas? They're pretty cheap as well. I got twenty."

"So, you-" she stopped and put a hand to her head. "So, you got twenty tarantulas. Yes. Of course you did. What exactly did you do with the twenty tarantulas?"

"I've put them in Ben's flat. They're all over the place. By the time he's spent an evening there, he'll be completely used to them."

"And you thought that would be a good idea?"

"It's brilliant! It was your idea, anyway."

"Jeremy, I think they do it a little differently. It's always got to be a choice for the person. They must *choose* to handle the tarantula."

"Nah. That'd take too long. My way will be quicker. And more fun."

"You're such an idiot!" yelled Nerys. "It won't work at all. He'll see the first one and probably drop dead from the shock. We need to go and get them. Now."

CLOVENHOOF MET Nerys outside Ben's flat thirty minutes later.

"Interesting outfit," Clovenhoof remarked.

"Yes, well. I may not be as scared as Ben, but there's no way a tarantula will be running up my trouser leg."

"No, not with parcel tape wrapped round your ankles."

"Or going down my neck."

"No, I can see that. I'm curious, why have you even got a veil? If I knew you were hoarding bridal wear I'd have kept you those little horseshoes from when I did tap dancing classes."

"It's not a real veil," said Nerys. "It's for keeping flies off food. It will do for this though."

"Weapons too, I see."

"Well a dustbuster seems like the humane way to capture a tarantula if you don't want to touch it."

"And the lump hammer?"

"Backup."

THEY LET themselves in using the emergency key.

"Where do we look?" whispered Nerys.

"I looked this up," said Clovenhoof. "They like to find

somewhere warm and hidden. I'll check his box of dirty mags, you look in the airing cupboard."

Nerys made her way towards the bathroom, swiping the dustbuster protectively in front of her when she heard a key in the lock.

"Oh no," she breathed.

Ben entered the flat and looked from Clovenhoof to Nerys and back.

"What on earth are you doing?" he asked.

"It was an emergency," said Clovenhoof. "Nerys thought she heard a noise."

Ben's eyes narrowed.

"So she dressed up like a zombie bride beekeeper and broke in to investigate?"

"Bees! Yes!" yelled Nerys. "I thought I heard masonry bees. They can cause devastation if they get into your walls."

"Oh. Right. Well I've come home to have a lie-down because I'm not feeling too well. You can do battle with phantom bees if you want, but keep it down, I'm going to bed as soon as I've had something to eat."

"You getting something from the fridge?" asked Clovenhoof.

"Yeah, I've got a pork pie," said Ben. "You're not having any."

Nerys gave urgent questioning signals to Clovenhoof with her eyebrows.

He responded with some less subtle signals indicating that he'd put a tarantula inside the fridge.

Nerys was tempted to air some age-old signals to show exactly what she thought of this, but turned back to the immediate problem that Ben was pulling open the door of the fridge.

"No!" she shouted.

"What?"

"Feed a cold, starve a fever," she said. Everyone knows that. Looks like you've got a fever to me."

"What? I've got tennis elbow. I can eat what I like."

"You might have some bad pork pie. Imagine how much worse it would be to have tennis elbow with food poisoning!"

"It's fresh, I bought it yesterday. I don't know why you think I'm such a slob that I can't keep a fridge of decent food. Look! It's all fine."

Ben stood aside with a flourish to show her the inside.

Nerys saw a spider the size of her hand rearing up from the butter dish, exposing its fangs. She leaped forward and slammed the door.

"Chicken soup is better," she said. "Why don't I make some while you take a nice bath?"

She ushered a confused Ben to the bathroom, giving Clovenhoof a sharp kick as she passed him.

"I'll run the bath while Jeremy gets you a towel. From the airing cupboard."

"Will you two go away if I have a bath and eat some soup?" Ben asked.

"Yes," Nerys said.

BEN LAID himself back in the bath and thought that maybe this bizarre hijacking might work out all right. It was certainly relaxing to bathe his sore arm in warm water. He draped a flannel over his eyes and dazily listened to the voices coming through the thin wall.

"I'm going to look it up on the internet," said Nerys.

"You need patience," said Clovenhoof.

"Patience? We only found one of them so far. Yes, put that one in the jar. There must be some other place that we haven't thought of yet."

"Don't panic. As long as we find them before Ben then it'll be fine."

Ben grunted to himself. Why did they need to find masonry bees before he did? It's not like he had spiders in the walls. He shuddered involuntarily, blindly reached for the bath scrunchie with one hand, the fat bar of soap with the other and started to lather up.

"Here's a discussion thread," Nerys was saying. "It seems as though we're not the first people to lose them in the house. We might be the first to mislay twenty though."

"Dark, humid places are favourites," said Clovenhoof.

"Oh here's someone saying 'try this.'"

"Try leaving a dish of water out. Sooner or later it will get thirsty and you can lure it out."

"Maybe they've gone off in search of drink already."

"Somewhere, wet, dark and humid."

There was a moment's silence and then Nerys and Clovenhoof cried out at once. There was a bang and crash as the bathroom door was forced in.

Ben leapt to his feet, the flannel falling from his eyes as he covered his naked manly bits with the foamy scrunchie.

"What the buggering hell do y-"

He froze.

For a mere fraction of a second he wondered if he had bought a new floral patterned shower curtain without realizing. And then he saw that those eighteen shapes were not flowers but hairy long-leggedy things.

He took a deep breath, readying to scream, but then a little corner of his brain did a recount. Eighteen shapes. *They* had lost twenty, they said. They had put one in a jar. And there was his blue scrunchie hanging on the cold water tap, dry and untouched.

Ben looked down at the soapy hairy thing he had pressed against his groin. A soap bubble burst on one its eight eyes. The tarantula wriggled angrily.

And then the screaming began in earnest.

7

A CAT IN HELL'S CHANCE

Rutspud scampered over the hot rocks to catch up with Slugwrench.

"What is it?" he asked for the third time.

"Can't tell you," said Slugwrench, his punctured lung wheezing and spitting like an asthmatic bagpipe. "Must show you. It's over here."

If friends were permitted in that place, Slugwrench would have been one of Rutspud's best friend. As it was, Slugwrench was his favourite enemy, his least hated rival. Sure, Slugwrench was a bit too career focussed, too keen to climb that greasy pole (the one with venomous lobsters and angry dentists at the bottom) but he had a pleasant streak of individuality and, besides, Rutspud couldn't help but respect a fellow who wore his major organs on the outside of his skin with such panache.

Rutspud followed him around a lake of lava and through a copse of razor-sharp stalagmites.

"I don't usually come out this way," he said.

"Have they still got you working with the fornicators?" said Slugwrench.

Rutspud gave a bitter laugh.

"There's so many of them, we've had to subdivide them. I work with the 'but I was drunk, I didn't mean it' lot. It's tough work but some of the stories you hear... *This* is new."

He stopped at the edge of a chasm and looked down into the gloom.

"The Pit of Pride and Vanity," said Slugwrench, apparently glad for the opportunity to stop briefly. His little heart, perched on top of his shoulder, was pulsating like a disco-dancing tumour. "It's always been there."

"I know that," said Rutspud. "I remember them, crawling around naked on all fours, trying to catch a glimpse of themselves in the jagged shards of mirror. Bloody hilarious. Literally. No, I meant these," he said and pointed at the cameras positioned around the walls.

"Oh, they *are* new," said Slugwrench. "It's the newer residents. Very sad cases. We're thinking of renaming it the Reality Television Pit. Listen. You can hear them."

Rutspud strained his huge ears.

A string of reedy voices could just be heard far below in the murk.

"I really think I've got what it takes to make it to the next level..."

"I can be whatever I want to be as long as I hold on tight to my dreams and follow my lucky star..."

"I'm a unique and special snowflake. I'm a unique and special snowflake. I'm a..."

Rutspud pulled back in horror.

"They've snapped. You've been too harsh on them."

Slugwrench gave Rutspud a look.

"We don't do anything to them. We've even got rid of the broken glass."

"You mean they're like that normally?"

"Oh, you've not even heard the ones who narrate their own lives. Sickening. But that's not what I wanted to show you. Come on."

Rutspud allowed himself to be pulled on. Behind him, one voice could still be heard.

"Day eight hundred in the pits of Hell. Marco decides to tell Chelsea how he feels about her..."

They continued onward through red caverns and up onto a high, frozen plateau.

"Oh, I know this place," said Rutspud. "The Plains of Leng, isn't it?"

"Shhh," said Slugwrench. "Shush and listen."

Rutspud stood still and did as instructed. The frigid wind whistled around them. Cold, dead stars that were definitely not stars wheeled above them.

Rutspud was about to ask what he was meant to be listening for when he heard it.

A small, pitiful yowl echoed from ahead.

"What is it?" said Rutspud but Slugwrench simply waved him forward.

The sound had come from a hole in the ground.

"I heard it the other day," said Slugwrench. "I don't know what it is."

They gathered around the narrow-mouthed opening and looked down. The thing in the hole cried out again.

"Is it in pain?" said Rutspud.

"I don't think so," said Slugwrench. "It's hard to see under all that fur."

"Maybe it's a plea of some sort."

"It wants something?"

Two yellow eyes in the mass of white fur looked up at them.

"What could it possibly want?" said Slugwrench.

"A shave?"

Slugwrench shook his head.

"I thought it might be a warning cry. A foreboding."

"Like a banshee?"

"Mmmm."

"What's it warning us?"

"It keeps saying, 'Mao.' I wondered if it was trying to tell us something about Mao Zedong."

"Like what?"

"Maybe something bad is about to happen to Chairman Mao."

Rutspud thought on that.

"Worse than what we're already doing to him? That'd be tricky."

Slugwrench gave an exasperated shrug, a gesture leant extra emphasis by his surprisingly expressive liver.

"But what is it?"

Rutspud looked closely.

"It's small but its head is like that of a manticore."

"Ah. I thought it looked like the demon queen Bast."

"I know what you mean. But it has the body of a sphinx."

"I've not seen anything like it."

"Nor me."

Slugwrench squatted on the ground, careful not to sit on his kidneys.

"Is it a resident?"

Rutspud was doubtful.

"Look at those eyes. I think it's one of us."

The creature yowled at them again.

"It clearly wants something," said Slugwrench, "but what? I don't know if we should ignore it or not?"

After a long pause, Slugwrench looked at Rutspud.

"That's why I asked you here."

"Me?"

"You're the clever one."

"Am I?"

"I wear my brain as a sporran, Rutspud. Yes, you're the clever one."

"What about Bootlick? He's smart."

"He'd just say we should eat it."

"True. That is his answer to everything."

"I thought I ought to take it to The Boss," said Slugwrench.

"Woah, now," said Rutspud, holding his hands out in warning. "You don't just take things to The Boss. What if it's a bad thing? What if he blames us for it?"

"Well maybe not The Boss but someone in charge? Berith?"

"Who would eat both it and us."

"Azazel?"

"Have you forgotten what he did to those demons who let Dante Alighieri escape?"

"Well, what then?" said Slugwrench, nervously tying knots in his dangling loops of intestine.

Rutspud thought for a minute and then clicked his fingers.

"We take it to the wisest resident and ask him."

"The wisest resident? As in... the Oldest Resident?"

Rutspud nodded.

"But he's scary!" said Slugwrench.

"He's a frightening piece of work, I admit, but at least he won't eat us, flail the skin from our backs or grind us in the Bosch power-mincer."

Slugwrench clearly saw the sense in this. There was the matter of how to transport the thing in the hole to the Oldest Resident. Neither of them was keen to touch it. In the end they agreed that Rutspud would hoist it out and Slugwrench would carry it.

Rutspud crouched down, reached into the hole and scooped his hand under the thing's belly.

"Uugh! It's so fluffy!" he said, fighting back his gag reflex.

The thing mewed at him and wiggled its stumpy little legs as he drew it out.

"Here!" he said, thrusting the thing at Slugwrench. "Oh, Hell. It's got little whiskers and a tiny button nose. Yuck!"

Slugwrench pulled aside a huge flap of skin on his side and bundled the thing up in it. He shuddered briefly at its touch. His stomach groaned and spat out a wad of black bile in protest.

"Come on," he said.

Rutspud led the way down from the Plains of Leng and across the Fields of Abbadon. As a shortcut that would hopefully avoid encountering any of the lords of Hell, the pair of them nipped through the Hall of Angry Bigots.

Rutspud thought it a shame that they didn't have time to linger as the Angry Bigots were always fun. Every time one of them started to say, "I'm not a racist, but..." an imp would leap in and jab its pitchfork up their racist butt. And whenever any of the residents tried to blame their woes on the 'bloody immigrants' a clerical devil would give them a five hour lecture on how, in this place, *everyone* was an immigrant and then brand the word 'immigrant' on them with a white-hot iron. What entertained Rutspud so much was the fact that, even after decades and centuries of torture, they never learned.

Beyond the hall, they skirted round the base of the Hill of Sisyphus. The ancient king of Ephyra huffed and puffed as he toiled high above them.

"Blimey, listen to him," said Rutspud. "Making a bloody meal of it."

"I'd be more than grunting if I was eternally damned to push a rock up a hill, only for it to roll down again," said Slugwrench.

"Yeah? Have you seen that rock though? It used to be the size of a house." Rutspud looked up at Sisyphus nudging the football-sized rock with his foot.

"That's just three thousand years of natural erosion," said Slugwrench. "Give the man a break."

"He's a tosser."

"You're just sore because he beats you at poker."

Rutspud fell silent, partly because Slugwrench had hit upon the truth, partly because they now stood at the entrance to the cave of the Oldest Resident. An impossible wind blew from its dark mouth, a wind both bitingly cold and cloyingly hot.

"I don't want to go in there," said Slugwrench, his arms tightening around the skin-wrapped creature, which squeaked in response. "I'm frightened."

"Are you a coward?" said Rutspud, who didn't really want to brave the cave either.

"A lily-livered coward," said Slugwrench and waggled his liver at Rutspud as evidence.

"Remember," said Rutspud, "he can't hurt us."

"I know. I know. But he *looks* at you."

"It's this or The Boss, buddy."

"Fine, fine."

Side by side, they edged into the darkness

Rutspud wished that handholding between demons wasn't a taboo, one punishable by a session with the thumbscrews, and was silently relieved when Slugwrench plunged his claws into the flesh of Rutspud's shoulder and drew closer.

At the end of the cave was an unexceptional cavern and, at its centre, the Oldest Resident on his throne of punishment. There were no chains or shackles but both demons knew that the Oldest Resident could never step from that throne. Beneath his soot black rags, a patchwork of wounds, scars and blisters marked out the aeons of torture he had suffered.

The Oldest Resident watched them approach. They

stopped at a very respectful distance, at the edge of the scorch marks and dried blood.

"Hello, sir," said Rutspud timidly and then coughed. "I mean, damned puny mortal."

"Hi," said Slugwrench, peering from behind Rutspud.

"Rutspud," said the Oldest Resident in a leaden voice. "Slugwrench."

Rutspud quivered at the sound of his name. The Oldest Resident knew him, remembered him. What did it mean? What power did it give him?

"What is it?" said the Oldest Resident.

"We have brought something to show you," said Rutspud and, with much prodding and faffing, had Slugwrench place the furry white creature on the floor.

"What new torture is this?" said the Oldest Resident, a strange smile appearing at the corner of his mouth.

"We hoped you could tell us, sir, I mean, most wretched of sinners."

"You mean, you don't know?"

Rutspud and Slugwrench exchanged looks.

"Er, no," said Slugwrench.

"Ah," said the Oldest Resident. "I must admit I haven't seen one in millennia. What you have there is the strangest of mythological beings, a 'cat'."

"Cat?"

"Or to be more specific, a 'kitten'. How did you come to find such a thing?"

"We found it," said Rutspud.

"*I* found it," said Slugwrench, suddenly emboldened.

"We were wondering," said Rutspud. "Well, we were wondering, what it's for?"

"What it's for?" said the Oldest Resident.

"Is it a good thing or a bad thing?"

"A deep question."

"Is it dangerous?"

The Oldest Resident drummed his fingers on the arm of his throne.

"People live in its thrall, compelled to serve its every whim."

The 'kitten' on the floor miaowed.

"That is the signal that it wants something," said the Oldest Resident, "and even the most wise and brave of the living run to fulfil its wishes."

"What does it want?" said Rutspud nervously.

"Tell us!" begged Slugwrench. "We don't want to incur its wrath!"

The Oldest Resident hummed to himself and continued to tap at the arm of his throne.

"Milk and fresh meat would be my guess."

"Fresh meat?" said Rutspud. "Where in Hell will we find that?"

Slugwrench, panicking, snapped off his own thumb and threw it at the kitten's feet. The bundle of fur sniffed at the gnarled digit and then nibbled it tenderly.

"I'm off to find Ceto," said Slugwrench.

"Ceto?" said Rutspud.

"Mother of a thousand demons. She must be lactating, surely?"

Slugwrench scampered off.

"I wonder how it ended up here," said the Oldest Resident.

"It's not a devil then, sir?" said Rutspud.

"Not in the sense you're thinking."

"I've never seen anything like it. Its hide looks all spiky but it's soft and warm like human innards. It has teeth and claws and cries like a wounded thing and yet the creature is perversely..." Rutspud groaned as language failed him. "I don't know the word to describe it."

"Cute," said the Oldest Resident.

"Cute?" said Rutspud. He had never heard the word before.

"The kitten is cute."

Rutspud shivered.

"It *is* cute," he said. "I hate it."

The kitten worked the finger down to the bone. The Oldest Resident patted his throne. Slugwrench returned with half a human skull filled with milk. He placed it on the floor and backed off quickly.

"Is it happy now?" he asked worriedly. "Are we safe from it?"

The Oldest Resident shook his head.

"Feeding the kitten will only delay its attack."

"Attack?" squealed Slugwrench.

"It will select one of us for its torture," said the Oldest Resident.

"How?"

The kitten stopped drinking, licked its face with a *cute* pink tongue and then walked over to the Oldest Resident's throne.

"Oh, no," said the Oldest Resident, still tapping the arm of his throne. "It appears to have selected me."

"Is there nothing we can do to stop it?" asked Rutspud.

"Nothing," said the Oldest Resident.

The kitten hunkered down and then jumped up into the Oldest Resident's lap.

"What is that noise it is making?" said Slugwrench fearfully.

"It is like the roaring of distant machines," said Rutspud.

"Like the rumbling of an empty stomach."

The Old Resident began to stroke the kitten's fur as it trod a circle in his lap.

"It is called purring," he said. "The torment is about to begin."

Slugwrench clung to Rutspud for comfort.

"If I stroke its fur, it might be merciful to me," said the Oldest Resident uncertainly and tickled the kitten under its chin.

"What should we do?" said Rutspud.

"Run," said the Oldest Resident, "or else the sight of my tortures might cause your heads to explode."

"Can that happen?" said Rutspud.

"I bet it can," said Slugwrench.

The kitten settled, wrapped itself into a ball and laid flat in the Oldest Resident's lap, purring.

"The lull before the storm," said the Oldest Resident. "Quick! Flee!"

The two demons needed no further exhortation and fled.

"Bring meat and milk tomorrow!" the Oldest Resident

called after them. "To appease it, lest it turns on you! It knows your scent now!"

From far up the tunnel came two terrified whimpers.

The Oldest Resident looked down at the kitten in his lap and stroked it with fingers that had long forgotten how to feel. He wept silently at the old sensation. The horrors of Hell seemed oddly distant now.

He wasn't going to question how or why the kitten had come to this place. Cats, like hell itself, were a law unto themselves. There was no point in questioning the ways of cats. There was no need.

"Hello, puss," he smiled.

But the kitten was already asleep.

8

THE NON-SPECIFIC PRAYER ASSESSMENT UNIT

Saint Christopher, former saint of travel, glared at the sea of heads that all swivelled in his direction as he entered the open plan office.

"Yes, yes. New boy in't job. Get back to yer own work," he called above the chatter.

"Now Christopher," said the Archangel Gabriel, steering him to a workstation, "it's very important that we convey a sense of calmness to our callers. I do hope that you can modify your tone when you begin your work here."

"I think you'll find that I've been answering prayers since most of these were in nappies," cried Christopher, casting an arm across the rows of seated operators. "Sorted everyone's travel arrangements, and their toothaches as well. There's nothing I don't know about answering prayers."

"Yes, well we do things a little differently here," replied Gabriel. "We might have to break a few bad habits."

"Bad habits? Now you listen to me, the only reason I'm

here is because some daft old sod who happens to be pope has declared that I never existed. It's all a misunderstanding, I'm certain. As soon as people realise that I'm not there for them, there'll be such an uproar that I'll be listed again, you'll see."

"Oh, but you will be there for them," said Gabriel. "In a sense. The calls for Saint Christopher are all now routed here, and any one of these operators is trained to respond in the appropriate manner."

Christopher shook his head sadly.

"The Non-Specific Prayer Assessment Unit provides a vital service," said Gabriel. "As we like to say, we're the people you call when you don't know who to call."

"How the Almighty can dump me – me! - in the ohgodohgodhelpmehelpline I will never know. Do you know who I am? Do you know who I am? I was fording mighty rivers in the good old days, carrying the weight of Our Lord on me shoulders."

"No, you weren't," said Gabriel. "That's the point. Besides we don't call it the ohgodohgod – and so on. This isn't a trivial service. All of these calls are important and must be taken seriously. You'll find the user guide and the online help will tell you exactly what to do. There's a script for every eventuality."

Gabriel handed him an enormous book, entitled *Quick reference to non-specific prayer scenarios*. Christopher took a seat and looked around. When they'd told him he'd be working in a call centre, he'd vaguely imagined that he'd be answering prayers as he used to, but sporting a natty headset like a rock star. He was beginning to realise that this was very different. He opened the quick reference at a random page. It was headed *"God! It's my husband. Get in the wardrobe!"* He groaned at the dense text below, packed with lines that he was supposed to read out. He flicked over the page to *"Jesus, I thought the handbrake was on"* and slammed the book shut with a bang.

"Well if you're ready to put on your headset, let's see you take a call," said Gabriel. "This is one is from Gavin in Essex who's hit his thumb with a hammer."

"God Almighty!" came the voice through the headset.

Christopher rolled his eyes.

"Hit his thumb with a hammer? Really? That's so stupid, I thought it only happened in cartoons."

"Stupid? I'll tell you what's stupid," said Gavin over the phone, "what's stupid is nagging your husband to put up a photo of your bloody family when he's been to the pub. Think I might give them all specs and moustaches, couldn't make them any uglier."

Gavin rang off, leaving Christopher staring in surprise at Gabriel.

"He could hear me! I mean properly hear me."

"He heard it as an inner dialogue," said Gabriel. "As far as he's concerned those words came from his own mind, his conscience. I told you we do things a little differently here. Now that was a very poor performance Christopher. You'll need to pay more attention to what you say to callers. Let's try another call. This one is Sandra in a situation we um, get quite often."

Christopher heard a woman's voice, breathing hard.

"Oh God," she gasped.

Christopher pulled a face and started to remove his headset, but Gabriel placed a firm hand over his.

"Oh what am I supposed to do here?" Christopher asked. He shrugged and then bellowed enthusiastically into the mouthpiece.

"Come on, love! Come on! It's just what you like, oh yeah!"

Sandra's breathing became more rapid, and Christopher took that to mean that his efforts were working.

"Yes! Oh yes," he roared. "Come on Sandra, come on girl! Atta girl!"

He had his eyes squeezed shut now, and concentrated hard on getting Sandra over the finishing line, shouting more urgently and punching the air as the pace quickened.

"Go Sandra! Give it all you've got girl! Nearly there now!"

Sandra rang off as she sighed with contentment after her climax, and Christopher opened his eyes to find an incredulous audience staring at him. Gabriel looked furious and the operators for several rows had abandoned their own calls to watch.

"Back to work everyone," snapped Gabriel. "We were all new once."

There was a muted grumbling noise and everyone shuffled back to their positions.

"Now, Christopher, that really isn't what we're here for," said Gabriel.

"I almost enjoyed that," said Christopher.

"If you'd taken a look at the online prompts you'd have seen that Sandra has left something cooking on the stove.

You were supposed to react to that and remind her. Now she's sleeping blissfully, the spaghetti will be ruined."

Christopher wondered whether this was entirely the right approach, but he answered the next few calls more carefully, reading the help text and checking the online prompts.

He felt he was getting into his stride when he took a call from Pat in Doncaster.

"God it hurts!" came a muffled scream.

"The pain will pass," soothed Christopher. He had learned some of the stock answers by now. "Try to picture yourself in a happy place."

"Hnyah! Got to *push* but it *hurts*!" howled Pat. "It's never going to come out!"

Christopher stiffened, suddenly gripped by the realisation that he was part of something amazing. He'd been patron saint of toothache before the papal decree, as well as his better-known duties for travel, but he'd never assisted with this sort of crisis before.

"Listen to your body Pat," he advised. "Push if you need to. Try to relax as much as you can in between pushes."

Christopher listened to Pat's laboured breathing slow very slightly and knew that he was helping. He tried some of the lullabies that he used to use for tired children on long journeys, and found that Pat reacted with quieter moans for a while.

"Need to go again, ohhh!" came the cry.

"You push if you need to, Pat. I'm here to help you. We'll take as long as you like," said Christopher.

The Archangel Gabriel came and tapped something on

the screen, but Christopher batted him away, knowing he'd got everything in hand.

"Pat, I know you just want the pain to stop, but you've got to remember, it'll all be worth it in the end."

Christopher was on a roll, he knew that Pat was coping much better with the pain thanks to his efforts.

"Can I just mention that Christopher is a really nice name?" he added quietly. "In case you needed one."

"Gahhh!" came the loudest roar yet, and Christopher sensed that Pat was making the final push, so he murmured soft encouragements, trying to get through the pain to the part of Pat's brain that was hearing his words. He ignored Gabriel, who was trying to get his attention again. Pat needed him more than Gabriel did right now.

Pat's shouting stopped, and there was a distinct *plink* from the other end of the phone line.

"Are you all right, Pat?" asked Christopher, puzzled.

He got no direct reply, but he heard a voice calling out just before the call ended.

"Hey, Maureen, I've passed the kidney stone. It's a whopper this one! Not sure why, but I think I'm going to call it Christopher."

9

THE HOOF

Nerys battered on Clovenhoof's door. When he opened it, she strode in, not giving him a chance to find an excuse to close it again.

"Did I just see Graham and Mark come in here?" she asked, peering around.

"Lovely to see you too, Nerys," said Clovenhoof.

A head popped round the bedroom door. It was at the level of Nerys's waist, so she put her hands on her hips, knowing that she was right.

"Hi Nerys," said Graham, "we're just getting our outfits on."

"Outfits?"

"Just wait until you see them!" called Mark.

Nerys gave Clovenhoof a look.

"You take advantage of those two!" she hissed. "I'm sure it's against the law, or the Geneva convention or something to mock gentlemen of limited stature."

"I'm not mocking them," said Clovenhoof. "I'm employing them."

Nerys narrowed her eyes at Clovenhoof and then widened them as Graham and Mark emerged from the bedroom in leather thongs. They were oiling up each other's torso with well-practised efficiency.

Nerys swallowed, as she remembered the time she'd woken up after a drunken fling with the energetic duo. They were quite something.

"What do you mean employing them?" she asked.

"I have a job today. As a matter of fact it's one that I must thank you for," said Clovenhoof. "Graham and Mark are my assistants for a wedding performance that is taking place."

Nerys thought for a moment.

"Does this have anything to do with the lookalike convention that we went to?" she asked.

"The one where you were hoping to pull men, but you were too tight to pay the ticket price?" asked Clovenhoof.

"Yes, well I was very disappointed in their George Clooney," said Nerys, "sixty-five if he's a day. As for their Leonardo di Caprio, he had acne like you couldn't imagine. I can't believe people would book such terrible lookalikes. It could only happen if they'd never actually seen them."

"I think that might happen sometimes," said Clovenhoof pointedly.

"No, wait," said Nerys. "We only put you down as *talent* so that we could get in for free. You didn't go round handing out leaflets or anything, so how did anyone ever book you?"

"It seems as though the names and contact details of the *talent* are emailed round to everyone who signs up for the mailing list," said Clovenhoof. "So, *The Hoof* has been booked to burst out of a cake and perform a song and dance routine at a wedding."

"They booked you as a David Hasselhoff lookalike?" asked Nerys, incredulous. "But we only put that down as a joke!"

"It seems as though they originally booked a Miley Cyrus lookalike, but they had to cancel because the insurers won't cover twerking injuries. They were really grateful to find a last minute substitute," said Clovenhoof.

"Oh surely you're not going to do it?" cried Nerys. "The most important day of someone's life and someone who looks nothing like David Hasselhoff is going to jump out of their cake and exploit dwarves in front of them?"

"That's gentlemen of limited stature to you, Nerys," said Graham.

"Sorry. I was forgetting myself," said Nerys. "It happens sometimes in the face of mind-boggling stupidity. Don't tell me you think this is a good idea?"

"Hey," said Mark, easing his buttocks into place after applying more oil. "Anything with a fee of two thousand pounds is a good idea, don't you think?"

Clovenhoof looked smug as Nerys stared at him slack-jawed.

"Well," she said, recovering rapidly. "You'll need someone to drive you there, and more importantly, get you out quickly afterwards. Can I suggest that you send Ben in ahead, as your agent?"

"Why?" asked Clovenhoof.

"You're going to want paying up-front, I reckon," said Nerys, and went off to get Ben.

BEN STOOD at the back of the room as the wedding party were seated for their meal. It was a large stylish room and Ben had the uncomfortable feeling that even the waiting staff thought he was making the place look untidy. He consoled himself with the fact that he had successfully extracted the fee from the bride's father . His job was done and he just needed to wait for Clovenhoof's performance.

Nerys slipped into place beside him.

"I've parked the rental van outside the front entrance," she whispered. "If things get ugly we can be out of here in seconds."

Ben nodded in approval.

The seated guests were arranged on tables in a horseshoe shape, leaving a large open space in front of the top table. The cake stood at the top of this space, at the focal point just in front of the bridal party.

"Have you seen the bride and groom?" hissed Nerys. "It's all very well having an eighties theme, but they've dressed up like Adam Ant and Madonna. I'm embarrassed for them, really I am."

"Does Jeremy have to wait in the cake until the end of the meal?" whispered Ben.

"Yes," said Nerys. "I really hope, for everyone's sake that he doesn't get bored in there."

Graham and Mark stood nearby, and Ben turned as he heard a crackle of static coming from their direction.

Graham lifted a walkie-talkie to his ear and muttered a brief response.

Ben nudged Nerys.

"Is Clovenhoof talking to Graham?" he asked, indicating with his head.

Nerys shrugged, and they both watched as Graham walked over to a side table which held glasses of champagne. Waiters and waitresses were moving back and forth, serving dishes of food, so nobody paid any attention as he approached the cake carrying a glass. He picked up a small length of hose which was attached to the side of the cake and carefully poured the champagne into the end. He walked back to the table, put down the empty glass and returned to his place by Ben and Nerys.

"Unbelievable!" muttered Nerys. Ben suspected that Nerys was bitter because she wanted a glass for herself, but as self-appointed getaway driver was unable to indulge.

Moments later there was another crackle from the walkie-talkie and Graham was on the move again. This time he went to the drinks table and took an entire bottle of champagne from a cooler. He went to the cake and upended the bottle into the end of the hose. Nerys made small explosive noises of indignation at Ben's side.

By the time Graham was back with Mark, everyone had their meals, and there was a gentle background hubbub of conversation. Ben and Nerys clearly heard a loud belch from inside the cake. They stiffened, and their eyes met. They waited for a few seconds and then allowed themselves to breathe normally again. Apparently nobody else had noticed.

Ben decided that there was only one thing worse than Clovenhoof at his most disastrous, and that was *waiting* for disaster to strike, as it inevitably would.

The main course was brought round, and Graham delivered another bottle of champagne to the cake while everyone was distracted.

"Honestly!" said Nerys through gritted teeth. "He'll be completely bladdered. I wonder if he even realises it's not Lambrini? I'm surprised he's not bursting for the loo by now."

A short while later, as everyone was eating their desserts, and waiting for the speeches, there was another brief interchange between Clovenhoof and Graham. Ben noticed the expression on Graham's face change. He walked up to the table and took an empty champagne bottle. The floor was deserted, but Graham walked boldly across. He placed the empty champagne bottle on the floor by the cake and popped a different hose into the top. Nerys and Ben looked on in horror as they realised what was about to happen. Graham strutted forward and turned a cartwheel, bowing appreciatively towards a brief clatter of applause from the audience. A loud tinkling sound suddenly came from the direction of the cake as the bottle began to fill. Graham whooped loudly, gesturing for Mark to come and join him. They both performed acrobatics for a few minutes, encouraging the crowd to clap along with them. It was a valiant attempt to cover up the sounds made by Clovenhoof's urine splashing into the bottle, but Ben could hear it quite clearly and he could see from Nerys's face that she could too. The bottle started to overflow, and a puddle expanded away from the base of the cake. Graham and Mark eventually decided that their task was complete, and trotted away from the cake, taking the bottle with them. The crowd called for more, banging cutlery and hollering encouragement.

"I can't believe nobody noticed what he was doing!" Ben said to Nerys.

"They've all had quite a bit to drink. Easily distracted," said Nerys. "Look, they're starting the speeches now. We don't have too long to wait."

The father of the bride stood up and the room fell silent.

He was a large, whiskered man who spoke with pride and love about his daughter. Ben was so wrapped up in his anecdote about her eighth birthday party, that when Nerys nudged him in the ribs it was quite a shock.

"Look!" she said, pointing at the cake.

Ben could see something moving on top of the cake. The ornamental bride and groom figures turned around and raised up slightly.

"What is that?" asked Ben.

"He's installed a bloody periscope!" Nerys hissed in fury.

Ben gaped. It was true. The figurines came to rest as they faced the bride's father.

They watched for tense moments. The periscope tracked the speeches, but nobody else had noticed the small movements at the top of the cake. There was a loud wolf-whistle at the point where the groom thanked the bridesmaids, but it was met with nervous laughter, as diners looked around at each other, wondering which of them was the culprit. Only Ben and Nerys could pinpoint the source.

The best man's speech was last of all. It seemed to Ben

that it lasted for quite a long time, and several of the jokes were making the bride quite angry. He cringed for the best man and was grateful that he'd never have to do anything so awful as a best man's speech.

"Why doesn't he just wrap it up!" Nerys said between her teeth. "Nobody wants to hear that the groom fancies the bride's sister!"

A loud farting noise came from the cake. Ben and Nerys both stayed very still. There was a moment where everyone looked around at each other again, wondering where the noise had come from. Then the laughing started and soon everyone was in uproar. The best man decided to quit while he was behind and sat down.

Graham and Mark saw their cue and marched, in time with each other to the centre of the room. They bowed to the top table, bowed to all of the guests around the edges and then approached the cake. They wheeled it forward so that it was at the very centre of the room. A spotlight appeared, focussing on the cake. A drumroll sounded, and Graham and Mark urged the crowd to clap and cheer in anticipation. As the drumroll and the cheering reached a crescendo, the top of the cake flew off and Clovenhoof erupted out, clad in red lycra swimming trunks.

"Well the fake tan has taken," said Nerys. "That was a good idea of mine."

"Just because he's orange, doesn't mean he looks as if he belongs on Baywatch," said Ben. "He looks more like a massive Oompa Loompa."

Clovenhoof strutted before the crowd, who were still

making a lot of noise, but a small, hesitant questioning sound had replaced the previous hollering.

"Hoof! Hoof! Hoof!" shouted Graham and Mark.

The crowd took up the cry.

"Hoof! Hoof! Hoof!"

They looked at each other and shrugged as they shouted it, but they seemed happy to play along. Only the bride looked somewhat disgruntled at the spectacle before her.

Clovenhoof had a microphone, handed to him by Graham.

"Hoof! Hoof! Hoof!" he bellowed, punching the air. "It's a pleasure to be here to perform for you today."

Clovenhoof raised his arms, as the crowd cheered.

"Why are they cheering him?" asked Nerys, incredulous. "He's an orange, middle-aged guy whose paunch almost hides his trunks."

Ben shook his head. He didn't understand either.

"I'm booked as a David Hasselhoff lookalike," shouted Clovenhoof, "but nobody wants to hear those terrible songs that he did, so I'm going to do something different."

The bride stood up and started to shout something. Ben got the impression that she probably did want to hear the David Hasselhoff songs, but her voice was drowned out by the sound of a thumping bass intro.

Clovenhoof stomped his feet in time.

"We're going to do *Another One Bites the Dust,*" he said. "Join in everyone, and let's hear it for Graham and Mark!"

Another display of acrobatics from Graham and Mark got the crowd clapping loudly, while Clovenhoof started the song. Ben had to hand it to him - his singing voice was good, but he just wasn' t sure it was the right song to choose for a wedding.

Apparently the bride thought so too, Ben realised. She'd got up from her chair and was coming around the table, her face a mask of fury.

Clovenhoof was oblivious. He thrust his hips in time to the music, Graham and Mark writhing at his feet.

The bride rushed towards them, but skidded on something as she passed near to the cake and landed on her back, bringing the cake down as she flung out an arm.

"She slipped on Clovenhoof's puddle of wee! This is a new low," gasped Nerys.

The groom rushed towards his wife, whose hooped petticoat had become entangled in the remains of the cake. He grabbed her under the arms and then his own legs skidded out from underneath him. He landed with an audible thud, rolling on top of his wife who made muffled mewling sounds.

The music was switched off by hands unseen, and Clovenhoof turned towards the top table.

"Who turned that off?" he queried. "I think it's a little unfair to put a stop to the lovely couple's first dance. They seem quite keen to show off their moves."

The charmless best man approached Clovenhoof.

"Give me that microphone!" he said. "I think your performance is over."

"It went down better than your speech," said Clovenhoof. "Let's hear it for the happy couple's break dancing routine, everyone!"

To Ben's amazement, there was a brief smattering of

applause for the sorry couple who had just managed to regain their balance.

The best man snatched the microphone from Clovenhoof and walked forward, while addressing the crowd.

"I think it's time to get things back on track ladies and gentlemen. First of all. let's get everyone's glasses topped up, and then I think I can rescue the show with some show tunes, if you're all up for that? Waddaya say?"

Nobody showed any real enthusiasm for show tunes, but the best man pressed on and grabbed a bottle of champagne that he whisked back to the top table.

He started to croon *Well Hello Dolly* as he went.

"Quickly!" said Nerys. "Grab the others. I'll start the van!"

"What's the hurry?" asked Ben. "They all seem fine to me."

"They won't be in a minute," said Nerys. "That bottle is the one that Clovenhoof filled up."

10

CLOVENHOOF'S SHED

"It says '*Closed for Refurbishment*'," Clovenhoof said, peering at the sign on the door of the Boldmere Oak.

"I think Lennox the barman mentioned something last week..." said Ben.

"But we can go in though?" said Clovenhoof, a whining tone entering his voice. "Can't we?"

"Course we can't go in," said Nerys. "That's what closed means."

"But we're regulars! What is this 'refurbishment' thing anyway?"

"You know, new carpet, new chairs, a lick of paint."

They jostled each other at the door for a few minutes, trying to peer inside to see what was going on. There were vague shapes moving beyond the frosted glass.

"But why would they want to refurbish it?" said Clovenhoof. "What's wrong with the old furbs?"

"Apart from the old fashioned décor and the funny stains and the feeling that *anything* could be living under those dusty benches you mean?" Nerys said.

"Yeah, exactly my point," said Clovenhoof. "It's perfect as it is. I liked those stains. I drew a moustache on one and called it Filmore and talked to it when there was no one else around."

"Bet he never got a round in," said Ben.

"No, he didn't," said Clovenhoof and shook a sudden fist at the closed pub door. "Screw you, Filmore! I hope you rot in hell!"

"Come on, you loonies," said Nerys, dragging them gently away from their cherished local.

"But where am I going to get a drink?" Clovenhoof grumbled as they walked towards the Chester Road.

Ben smirked at Nerys.

"What?" said Clovenhoof.

"Don't forget that we were with you last week when you bought that jacket *just because* the pocket was big enough to carry a bottle of Lambrini," said Nerys.

"It was a nice coat."

"It was a ladies coat."

"With deep pockets."

"Let's face facts," she said. "You drink at home. You drink in the street. It's only a matter of time before that nice lady in the library works out that you aren't all that interested in mediaeval maps, but you just send her off on errands so you can sup booze."

"It's important for a man," Clovenhoof announced loudly, cutting her off, "to have a place where he can forget his domestic burdens. Where he can relax away from the pressures and duties that crowd his life."

Nerys snorted.

"It's true," said Ben. "Men need that space. It's vital for any relationship to include room for each person to be themselves."

Nerys turned a wagging finger towards Ben.

"You've been reading my Marie-Claire again!"

"Have not," said Ben, blushing deeply.

"Anyway, I don't know what the two of you are talking about, neither of you even has a woman."

She thought for a moment.

"Although I did see you borrowing a footpump from next door the other day."

"That was for the wheelbarrow," said Clovenhoof.

"Maybe it was," said Nerys, eyeing him sideways, "but if you were trying to get away from women then you both overlooked something important."

"What?" said Ben.

"You always go to the pub with me."

"And?" said Clovenhoof.

"*And* I am a woman."

Clovenhoof and Ben stopped and looked at each other.

"Nah!" they chorused and then carried on.

"What?" said Nerys, fixed to the spot.

The men walked on, oblivious to the fact that they had left her behind.

"Oi!" Nerys shouted, balling her fists.

They stopped and turned back to her.

"I am a woman!" she yelled.

"Obviously you're a woman," Clovenhoof said, rolling his eyes. "But not in the ways that matter. You're one of us."

Ben nodded sagely.

"One of us."

"An honorary bloke," said Clovenhoof, striding up to Nerys, slapping her on the back and grinning widely.

This blokey generosity washed over her and left her unimpressed.

"I *am* a woman."

"Sure, I mean you've got boobs and stuff, obviously, but let's look at the facts. You're loud."

"And aggressive," added Ben.

"And you definitely don't understand women. That makes you more blokey than Ben."

"Also," added Ben, "you do tend to make decisions with your, er, you know."

He waved vaguely at the area below Nerys's waist.

"You're a man through and through," said Clovenhoof cheerily.

"It's a blessing," agreed Ben.

Clovenhoof and Ben walked away, chatting, safe in the knowledge they had put Nerys's worries to rest. Meanwhile Nerys stood, still rooted to the pavement with her mouth open, aghast at her flat-mates' revelation.

"Seriously, Ben," said Clovenhoof, looping an arm over the other man's shoulder, "I am bloody bereft. The Boldmere was my home from home. My womb."

"We'll go to another pub."

Clovenhoof considered this.

"No. Feels wrong. It'd be like cheating on her."

"Cheating on your womb?"

"I need my man-space but, another pub…? No."

"My uncle Peter was a big angler," said Ben.

"Yeah?"

"Always used to say that fishing was the thing that kept his marriage going. The perfect solitude. Man-space. He'd go down to the canal every weekend and fish. A man at one with nature, his rod in his hand."

"Did he have a big rod?"

"Are you being rude?"

"No, no," Clovenhoof assured him. "Fishing. Mmmm. Sounds interesting."

BEN ANSWERED his flat door to find Clovenhoof glowering at him.

"Er, come in," he said, as Clovenhoof stalked across the carpet, trailing a strange smelling, olive-green weed behind.

"Fishing! What a ridiculous thing," Clovenhoof said, flicking a water beetle from his ear. "It's colder than it looks out there when you're soaking wet."

"Where's the rod I lent you?" Ben asked.

"Bottom of the canal. I dropped the Lambrini in the water and a duck came after it."

"What, so you tried to scare the duck away with the rod and dropped it in?"

"No, I had to go and have words with the duck. The rod fell into the water when I was trying to pull myself back onto the bank. I was going to try and find it, but there was a supermarket trolley in there and I got distracted."

Ben shrugged.

"No worries. I always hated fishing anyway."

Clovenhoof turned and scowled at him.

"So you made me go, just to check it's still crap? I can't imagine ever wanting to spend time by such slimy, cold water. I had a Lake of Fire once, you know. Amazing place. You could just roast yourself in perfect isolation. I've never seen anything so welcoming and pure since I came here."

Ben nodded.

"Yeah, some people on Jockey Road have got one of those outdoor hot tub things."

"What?"

"You know, hot bubbly jacuzzi thing."

Clovenhoof gave him a look he'd copied from Nerys. The one she used on people who sat at their table in the pub. Water continued to drip from his clothes.

"I'm talking about a Lake of Fire, Ben."

Ben gave him a snooty look back.

"I don't know what make it was, Jeremy. I think they're a terrible waste of energy, especially in the winter."

"I've no idea what you're on about."

"All I'm saying," said Ben, "is they're not very British. Men in this country tend to just make do with a garden shed."

Clovenhoof frowned.

"A shed?"

"Yeah. You know, a bit of extra storage."

"Hmm," mused Clovenhoof. "My skull collection is getting a bit too big for the bathroom."

"Well perhaps, or a place to get away from the house and

relax a bit. My granddad had a folding chair and kettle in his."

"Liking it. But instead of a kettle, a fridge."

"Fridge?"

"For the Lambrini."

"Yes, but it's got to be a practical space for gardening or woodwork or... we could have a sort of war-gaming area with storage for the miniatures, yeah."

"But definitely a fridge for the booze, yeah?"

Each was lost for a moment in a private reverie. They drifted towards the window and looked out across the back garden.

"How big is a shed?" asked Clovenhoof.

"About the size of that corner there, I reckon," said Ben.

"Well, what are we waiting for?"

"Hang on," said Ben. "You don't just put up a shed."

"What do you do?"

"We need to make sure it's okay with everyone else in the house. How about this, I'll check downstairs if you go and talk to Nerys."

"No problem. I'll talk Nerys round. No-one can resist me at my most charming," said Clovenhoof, strutting towards the door.

"Well, can I make a suggestion then?" asked Ben.

"Sure."

"Change your trousers before you go. Duckweed in the groin is definitely not charming."

Nerys opened the door.

"Come right in, I'm baking biscuits!" she beamed.

Clovenhoof followed her in.

"What are you wearing?" he asked.

"What do you mean?"

"You don't normally wear things with flowers on, or long skirts, and...what is that thing?" he flicked a finger at the ruffles of an elaborate apron.

Nerys gave him a coquettish spin.

"It's the sort of thing that a modest and feminine woman wears when she's baking biscuits," said Nerys, teeth slightly gritted, "which, as you know, is a traditional, *feminine* pastime."

She pulled a tray out of the oven, along with a lot of thick smoke. Small, pitted black mounds were fastened intractably to the baking trays.

"And they're biscuits, are they?" said Clovenhoof, inhaling the acrid smoke with pleasure.

Nerys tried to prise them off with a spatula. One pinged off and put a dent in the ceiling but the others wouldn't budge. She then turned the tray upside down and tried hitting it to release the biscuits. They stuck resolutely in place. She swore in a traditional and rather unfeminine manner and then bit her tongue.

"Perhaps I should bake fairy cakes instead," she said and gave a dainty laugh that held more than a hint of madness.

"Anyway," said Clovenhoof pointedly, "I came to see you because Ben and I want to build a shed in the garden.

"A shed?"

"Wooden building thing. Apparently, it's more British than a hot tub."

"How interesting," said Nerys. "What do you want a shed for?"

"Oh, you know. To have some chairs, sit outside, that sort of thing."

"A summerhouse, you mean!"

"Do I?"

"Absolutely. How lovely," said Nerys. "You'll need some help picking out something suitable and making it homely, of course. A woman's touch."

"Cool, well if you want to help then why don't you and Ben come round to mine for dinner tonight and we can talk about it? I went fishing, so I've got something in."

"Sounds great – what are we having?"

"Duck."

NERYS PULLED up in her car the following day as Ben and Clovenhoof waited on the pavement.

"Sorry I'm late," she said. "I had to take Twinkle to the vet."

"What's wrong with him?" Ben asked.

"Oh, nothing much," said Nerys. "He broke a tooth on one of my biscuits and had a bit of a choking fit. He's all fine now."

She carried Twinkle inside and joined them back at the car.

"Look at that, someone's left that filthy supermarket trolley on our path," said Nerys, indicating a hulk of slimy green rust with flies buzzing enthusiastically round it. "I'll ring the council later and get them to take it away."

"Don't worry, I'll take care of it," said Clovenhoof, sniffing the delicate scent of rotting pondweed with relish.

They pulled up a few minutes later in a car park.

"I hope their sheds look better than their building," said Clovenhoof. "It's a giant tin box. Why would we believe that they have *Everything for the Home and Garden* when they can't even be bothered to put up a proper building?"

Once inside, they walked along the aisles, checking out the hanging signs.

"Ooh, soft furnishings," said Nerys.

"Since when have you been into soft furnishings?" said Ben.

"Oh, I forgot to mention," said Clovenhoof. "Nerys OD'd on Barbie pills and has gone all girly."

"Pay no attention to Mr Grumpy," said Nerys, wrinkling her nose. "I'm going to take a look at throws and scatter cushions. I'll see you boys in a moment."

She sashayed down the aisle, humming a tune from The Sound Of Music as she went.

"Righto," said Clovenhoof, clapping his hands together. "A call of nature and then sheds."

"Okay," said Ben disinterestedly, whose attention had suddenly been caught by a tiny hobby drill with interchangeable attachments on a nearby shelf. It was on special offer.

"I've always wanted one of those," said Ben but Clovenhoof had already gone.

He picked the drill up and turned it over in his hands.

"Handy for buffing my miniature soldiers with the polishing wheel," he continued to himself.

He'd need different grades of buffer for his scale model militaria, something for lighter general work but also some precision accessories. There was no information on the box so he looked round for an assistant.

NERYS HAD FOUND the perfect curtains. They were, she told herself, feminine, floaty and just perfect for a summerhouse. They were also bright pink and she was convinced that if she was to pass herself off as a real woman – a lady even – then pink was the only colour for her. Tucking them under her arm, she sped through to shop to find the lads, so that she could show off her find.

She found Clovenhoof in an aisle marked 'Bathrooms'

"Jeremy, look what I found!"

She thrust the curtains towards him, but then pulled up short.

"What on earth are you doing?" she asked.

"What does it look like?" asked Clovenhoof, who was sitting on a display toilet with his trousers around his ankles.

"But, you can't do that," she shrieked. "This is not here for you to...use."

"That is clearly the case," said Clovenhoof, looking round. "The facilities are a bit lacking in the essentials. But I see you thought of that. Well done."

He took the curtains from her and raised a butt cheek with a satisfied sigh.

Nerys squealed and fled.

She found Ben talking to an ungainly youth.

"Can you tell me what accessories are available for this please?" Ben asked, holding out the hobby drill.

"'s there on the shelf," mumbled the youth.

Ben smiled politely.

"No, I can see what's there on the shelf, but there must be other things."

The youth gave him a perplexed look.

"Like spare buffers," said Ben.

The youth shook his head.

"Shelf," he grunted, motioning towards the shelf and backing away.

"No, it doesn't matter about the shelf," said Ben, stepping in front of him to block his path. "The manufacturers must have other things. I bet you have a catalogue that you order things from, don't you? Can we look at that?"

The youth eyed him with panic.

"Can you find someone else?" Ben tried. "A supervisor, perhaps?"

The youth nodded nervously and bolted around the corner.

Moments later he came back with an older man, who didn't have a smart uniform like the youth, who at least had a warm and avuncular smile for Ben and Nerys.

"I'm Sidney," he said as the youth sloped off. "Can I be of assistance?"

"Er, yes," said Ben. "I want to know if there are accessories available for this hobby drill."

Sidney pursed his lips and gave Ben a look.

"Well there are no accessories sold in this store, and the company's policy does not allow for one-off ordering."

"Oh."

"However, I can jot down the website of the manufacturer, which is excellent. There's also a small shop in Erdington that stocks the full range of accessories."

Sidney jotted down the details and handed the note to Ben.

"Wow," said Ben. "That's great, thanks."

"Is there anything else I can help you with today?" asked Sidney.

Ben thought for a moment.

"Well, actually, there is something. I was wondering whether it might be more economical to buy some of my enamel paints in larger tins like you have here. It all depends how it's formulated. It'll need to mix with my other paints."

"Would you like to study the Material Data Sheets?" asked Sidney.

Ben's face lit up with a smile so huge that Nerys didn't have the heart to grumble so she decided to go back to the soft furnishings.

A loud noise made her look across at a display of power tools. She saw that Clovenhoof had unplugged a computer terminal from a floor socket and had replaced it with the power lead to a large orange device that was bucking in his hands.

"What's that?" she yelled.

"A leaf blower," said Clovenhoof. "No leaves to try it on though."

He stretched the cord behind him to move around the corner. Nerys looked on in horror as a leaflet display exploded into the air, swirling higher, as Clovenhoof wielded the leaf blower with a whoop.

The power was cut suddenly, and Clovenhoof looked round in disappointment.

"Can I get you the box for that sir?" asked Sidney, handing Clovenhoof the plug. He was accompanied by Ben, who was studying a sheet of dense text.

"Yes please," said Clovenhoof. "Actually, there are some other things here that I need."

THEY MOVED into the outside area to look at the sheds. Sidney followed behind Clovenhoof with a hand truck piled high with power tool boxes.

"Jeremy, is that a chainsaw?" asked Nerys, peering at the stack of boxes.

"Yeah!" said Clovenhoof.

"I can't imagine what you'd want with a chainsaw," said Nerys.

"Well I don't know how I've gone for this long without one," said Clovenhoof. "I can imagine all sorts of things I want to do with it."

"How are you going to afford all of these things?" asked Nerys.

"No problem," said Clovenhoof. "I came into a bit of money the other day."

"Oh, really?"

"Yeah, I met someone running out of the Post Office. He tried to knock me over, so I thumped him. He hit me over the head with this bag and it got stuck on my horns."

Nerys's eyes flickered upwards. She frowned slightly, then shook her head.

"And then what?" she asked.

"He realised it was stuck so he ran off. When I opened it, there was loads of money inside."

"Really?"

"Yep."

"Oh, right." Nerys shrugged. "I guess we can afford a decent shed then?"

"Yeah. What about this one?"

They all stopped near to a large shed with an apex roof.

"No good," said Ben. "This one's not tanalised."

"What's that?" asked Clovenhoof.

Ben nudged Sidney, grinning gleefully at his new best friend. They leaned together and chorused as one. "It's treated inside a pressure vessel with a wood preservative called Tanalith."

Clovenhoof went misty-eyed for a moment.

"Tanalith," he said. "One of the most curvaceous demons you ever laid eyes on."

"Eh?" said Sidney.

"Acid flashback," said Ben to Sidney. "We think he did a lot of drugs in the sixties."

They moved on to the next shed.

"This one is better," said Ben.

Nerys pouted.

"Why do you want a boring square-shaped shed? Surely if we're going to sit outside in the sun, we should get one of those?"

She pointed to the window-fronted summerhouses.

"People can see inside," said Ben. That's not very secure, if we want to store valuable things like collectable militaria."

"Well there should be some windows," said Nerys. "Or where will we put the curtains?"

"As long as there's room for a fridge, it doesn't matter," said Clovenhoof.

They eventually agreed on a shed with shutters at the windows, and wheeled their purchases to the checkout. Clovenhoof piled on more tools and a remote controlled tank from a display mysteriously marked as 'seasonal' as they went.

"I'll just go and get someone to pop you through the checkout," said Sidney.

"Can't you do it?" said Ben, slightly disappointed.

"I'm afraid not," said Sidney. "I don't actually work here."

Sidney walked away and they all stared at his back for a long moment.

"Is that why they call it Do-It-Yourself?" asked Clovenhoof.

NERYS WOKE the next morning to the sound of hammering. She looked out of her window and saw Clovenhoof in the garden, tools and timber scattered everywhere. He was stripped to the waist, so she lifted the net curtain to take a discreet peek, but decided not to go down, in case she got roped in to help. She watched as Clovenhoof braced a panel against his shoulder so that he could fasten a bolt through to another piece. He lined it up and got the bolt through, but then realised that the spanner was just out of reach. She wondered whether to go and pass it to him as he wriggled and stretched to reach it. After a few moments, he decided to make a rapid dive for the tool box and leap back before everything fell to the ground, but he was too slow. Panels fell to the floor with a slap and Clovenhoof jumped up and down, swearing viciously.

BEN CAME HOME in the late afternoon and went out into the back garden to take a look at Clovenhoof's progress.

He squinted into the low sunlight, trying to see where Clovenhoof was. His foot clinked against an empty Lambrini bottle. He looked down and saw that there were many more. He followed the trail and found Clovenhoof snoozing against a stack of wood. In his hand he gripped a tool of some sort.

"Jeremy, I think you might want to wake up. If you're going to sleep, why not go inside?" Ben said, shaking Clovenhoof's shoulder.

Clovenhoof woke up with a shout, and sat bolt upright. His grip tightened on the trigger of the nail gun that he had clasped in his hand, firing a nail into Ben's foot.

Ben howled and rolled around on the grass. Within seconds, Nerys came scampering across the lawn with her first aid kit and a look of gleeful anticipation.

"What seems to be the matter?" she said, in a weirdly breathy voice which might have been an attempt to model her speech on that of Marilyn Monroe but, given the circumstances, made her seem like someone auditioning for a role in the porn version of the Florence Nightingale story.

"The bastard shot me!" Ben squealed.

She kneeled over Ben and pulled off his shoe, ripping the nail away with and eliciting more screams. His grubby white sock was rapidly becoming a soggy red sock and she dressed his foot quickly, shushing him gently all the while.

Clovenhoof staggered to his feet.

"People should know better than to disturb a man at work," he said. "Very dangerous."

"You were asleep!" yelled Ben. "Who sleeps with a loaded nail gun in their hand?"

"Someone who wants to put a shed together when he wakes up?" Clovenhoof said, peering at Ben's foot. "That looks nasty. You should get someone to look at it."

The looks that Ben and Nerys both gave him were wasted as he lay back down and started to snore gently.

NERYS HAD RESOLVED NOT to look out of the window. Every time she did, she saw some fresh horror, like Clovenhoof chasing Twinkle round the garden with his ridiculous leaf-blower, or wielding his chainsaw like a maniac. She was sure that there were expletives carved into the fence. It was quiet today though.

"Too quiet," she said to herself.

Twinkle, shell-shocked from the leaf-blower experience made sympathetic whimpers at her feet.

There was no hammering from outside, no roars of power tools. She decided to go down and have a look and found Clovenhoof by the fence.

"What are you doing?" she asked.

"Putting this tree back. The man over there got angry that I chopped it down with my new chainsaw."

"You can't put a tree back when it's cut down," said Nerys. "You're sticking branches to the fence. That's different."

"Well I had to use this glue gun, it's great. The tree will look the same to the guy over there. He'll never notice the difference."

"It's an apple tree, I think he might."

THE FOLLOWING DAY, Nerys was pleased to see that the stinking supermarket trolley had been removed. She locked the door of her car and a curious noise made her walk round to the access path between the houses. She leaped back as a nightmarish sight bowled along the path towards her. It looked for all the world as if someone had motorised a supermarket trolley and fitted a chainsaw to its prow. A miniature shed roof topped the monstrosity.

"Jeremy!" she yelled. "I know this is your doing! Come and stop this thing immediately!"

Clovenhoof emerged from the path as the trolley dashed into the road. He held a remote control in his hands, and shrugged at Nerys.

"I think it's got a really short range," he said. "I can't seem to control it."

"I don't want you to control it," she yelled. "I want you to stop it!"

It was careering up the road now, sending cars swerving as it rattled towards them. Clovenhoof ambled after it, admiring its trajectory and wondering why no modern, regularly-used supermarket trolley without a revving chainsaw and wooden roof would ever go in such a straight line. Eventually it went up a ramp onto the pavement and Clovenhoof sped up, thinking he might stop it shortly.

One of the wheels struck an edging brick and the trolley went into a spin. Clovenhoof stepped back as the chainsaw whipped towards him. It would be rather inconvenient to have his chest ripped open. The trolley sped off in a different direction and he sighed and broke into a trot. It was plummeting down a ramp now and he realised that it was heading directly for the canal. He lunged to grab it but wasn't quick enough. He sighed in disappointment as it sank below the surface. Nerys caught up a few moments later and watched with him.

"What possessed you? What on earth was that thing?" she asked.

"I saw a telly programme with fighting robots," he said. "That was my first attempt. I don't think it went too badly, all things considered."

"Well at least it's got some of your more dangerous toys out of the way," said Nerys, turning for home. Clovenhoof peered into the murky water for a while and decided that he could pull them back out another day. He walked off, idly wondering how big a remote controlled helicopter would have to be to carry a chainsaw.

ON SATURDAY AFTERNOON, Nerys went to help Ben with his crutches and they ventured outside together to take a look at the shed.

Clovenhoof dozed in a deckchair so they walked around quietly, checking out his handiwork.

"You know, this actually looks pretty good," said Ben, putting a spirit level over the door. "I've no idea how, but it all looks solid and square."

"Aren't the windows just crying out for those darling curtains that I bought?" squealed Nerys, clapping her hands together childishly.

That woke Clovenhoof, who stretched and grinned at them both.

"Barbecue tonight?" he said.

"Oh yes!" said Nerys. "I'll go and buy some things when I've put all the soft furnishings in here. I must get extra sausages for Twinkle, he loves a sausage."

She frowned.

"Where is Twinkle?"

That was when they heard it. A faint yipping sound coming from beneath the shed's wooden floor.

THE CURTAINS FLUTTERED at the windows as Clovenhoof brought in another armful of bottles to form his bar. Ben was busy setting up a wargaming table, and Nerys relaxed on a sun lounger on the veranda, with Twinkle cowering underneath. Clovenhoof stepped over to the barbecue and turned the sausages with a flourish.

"Who's for a hot dog?" he bellowed.

Twinkle whined from his hiding place.

"Sometimes I think he understands us, you know," said Nerys, getting up. "I'm going to light the candles before it gets dark. Some of them are scented. We've got Citronella to keep the bugs away, and Jasmine because it's so, so beautiful."

"How long are you going to keep this up?" asked Clovenhoof, rolling his eyes.

"Keep what up?"

"The awful pink girly bleating. The frilly aprons."

He pointed to the see-through organza curtains.

"A few weeks ago, you might have worn that as a dress with a bikini underneath, not hung it at the window."

He turned back to her.

"Is that, is that...embroidery?" he spluttered as she put something down on the table.

"Yes, I'm making a sampler," said Nerys.

"Let me see," said Ben, coming over. "You know that good embroidery should look as neat on the back as it does on the front?"

They turned over Nerys's work. It looked like a bird's nest on the underside.

"Ben!" sighed Clovenhoof. "I never thought I'd say this, but set up your wargaming table. Let's get this party started."

Two hours later Nerys had made use of all the empty Lambrini bottles, arranging them round the shed with candles on top of them, giving the place the air of a cheap Italian bistro. She lolled on top of a large beaded cushion while Clovenhoof and Ben stared at each other over the wargaming table.

Clovenhoof had decided to sample the spirits from his newly built bar. He was currently on vodka which he sipped from a brimming tumbler.

Ben had a small steel ruler in his pocket, and used it to

take measurements on the wargaming board. He pulled out of his pocket a pair of reading glasses and put them on to scrutinise the board from every angle.

"I never saw you wear glasses before," said Nerys.

"I only use them for close, precision work," said Ben.

While Ben agonised over his troop movements, Clovenhoof found himself drunkenly daydreaming of another battle, long ago. Not a silly battle with lead figures and nothing so mundane or two-dimensional as the skirmish playing out here on this unrealistic scale model field.

Clovenhoof remembered the broad heavens and the rows and rows of angels pitted against one another. He would have won too if the numbers had been on his side and he had not been blinded by the light. It was a close fought thing but also a crushing defeat followed by that slow, hard fall into the bowels of Hell and the Lake of Fire.

He smiled to himself. Funny how the Lake, his punishment for insurrection, was the thing he missed most about the Old Place now.

"I'm done," said Ben, straightening up.

Clovenhoof grinned boozily at Ben.

"Well, the numbers aren't on your side this time," he said.

"Eh?" said Ben.

"Not talking to you," said Clovenhoof.

Thirty seconds later, after screaming incoherent battle cries of revenge and getting a bad attack of the hiccups as a result, Clovenhoof had sent half of his tabletop army to their deaths.

"Those fallen trees are working against me," he grumbled.

"Those are sausages," said Ben eyeing Clovenhoof over the top of his reading glasses.

Clovenhoof grabbed all three cold sausages and stuffed them into his mouth at once, making feral chomping noises. He then sat back and belched in triumph. Nerys tutted loudly.

"So, what's your next move?" asked Ben.

Clovenhoof thought deeply. What an expert tactician needed was a brilliant move to swing the battle round in his favour, something truly unexpected...

He leaped up and grabbed his leaf blower.

"A hurricane!" he yelled, blasting soldiers from the board as he swung it wildly. He swung it again, to be sure that the battlefield was completely cleared. Tiny soldiers and salted peanuts were all swept away in a pleasing vortex of chaos.

"Now I understand the appeal of wargaming!" he yelled. "This is great!"

The tumbler of vodka was caught in the small-scale gale and tipped over. Tiny droplets of spirit blew across the shed as a mist, ultimately and unavoidably finding the candle flames. A small but impressive fireball lit up the shed, setting light to the highly flammable organza curtains.

Ben screamed and fled, tripping over Nerys's lounger and spilling them both into the garden.

Clovenhoof stayed where he was and stared in admiration at the flames that surrounded him. Finally, he had created a place that really felt like home! His glorious Lake of Fire was lost to him, but this reminded him so powerfully of its beauty that it brought a tear to his eye. He turned around slowly, lost in nostalgia.

"Jeremeee!"

Nerys plunged through the door and tugged his arm.

"Come on you fool, stop messing about!"

She hauled him out onto the lawn and collapsed, panting and coughing while Clovenhoof gazed at the fire with wistful regret.

"How drunk would you have to be to just stand there in a burning building?" she spluttered.

Ben gave her a tentative pat on the back as she coughed again and she glared at him.

"It was so hot. So beautiful," said Clovenhoof dreamily.

"Idiot," said Nerys, scrambling to her feet. "Wait, can you guys hear sirens? I think the firemen are coming!"

"So they should be," said Ben.

"Young, muscly, athletic firemen."

She looked down at her long tiered skirt and buttoned-up blouse. She unbuttoned the top half of her blouse, tousled her hair and ripped off her skirt above the knees. She threw the excess fabric onto the burning shed. As an afterthought she kicked a couple of scatter cushions after it.

"Now, where did I put my emergency lippy?"

"Hey Ben," said Clovenhoof, throwing an arm over his shoulder. "We may have lost our nice new shed, but at least Nerys is back to normal! Everything's going to be fine."

ABOUT THE AUTHORS

Heide Goody is the stupid one in the writing partnership and Iain Grant is the sensible one. Together they are the authors of numerous novels and two short story collections.

They run workshops and attend genre events in the UK.

You can often find them on Facebook sharing silly pictures and harvesting jokes to put in their novels.

Heide and Iain are both married but not to each other.

You can sign up to their author newsletter to find out about upcoming events and new books.

And the archangel Michael constantly snooping on him, doesn't help.

If you enjoy clever writing, then you'll adore this satirical tour de force, because a good laugh can make you have sympathy for the devil.

Get it now.

Clovenhoof

Oddjobs

Unstoppable horrors from beyond are poised to invade and literally create Hell on Earth.

It's the end of the world as we know it, but someone still needs to do the paperwork.

Morag Murray works for the secret government organisation responsible for making sure the apocalypse goes as smoothly and as quietly as possible.

Trouble is, Morag's got a temper problem and, after angering the wrong alien god, she's been sent to another city where she won't cause so much trouble.

But Morag's got her work cut out for her. She has to deal with a man-eating starfish, solve a supernatural murder and, if she's got time, prevent her own inevitable death.

If you like The Laundry Files, The Chronicles of St Mary's or Men in Black, you'll love the Oddjobs series.

"If Jodi Taylor wrote a Laundry Files novel set it in Birmingham... A hilarious dose of bleak existential despair. With added tentacles! And bureaucracy!" – Charles Stross, author of The Laundry Files series.

Oddjobs

Sealfinger

Some bodies just won't stay buried.

When a client tells Sam Applewhite she's seen ghosts in the
nearby graveyard, Sam dismisses it as the ramblings of an old
woman. She's got bigger things to worry about — keeping on top
of her job at DefCon4 Security Services isn't easy — particularly
since her manager is a cactus and no one will tell her what her job
actually is.

But when the ghost-spotting client goes missing and only Sam
suspects foul play, she is compelled to dig deeper.

Aided by her retired stage magician father and the owner of the
most outlandish junk shop on the sea front, Sam dives into a
mystery involving psychotic seals, unexploded air force
munitions, DIY foot surgery and a corpse that just won't quit.

Sealfinger